Touch Not

By

George V. Henderson

*To Donna*

*Best Wishes !*

The Publisher

*September 19, 2006*

First Published 2003
by The Publisher

ISBN 0-9685032-7-6

This book is dedicated to Louise and Victor
Znack for their support and love and to
David McKeown for all his help
and friendship.

The Publisher
17-700 Mcleod Rd., Suite 272
Niagara Falls, Ontario, Canada
L2G 7K3

Printed in Canada by The Publisher
Niagara Falls, Ontario

# Chapter one - 9:33 Am, San Terriora El Terra, Central America

## Rain

The rain didn't fall, it slashed, hacking at the sides of the white stucco house. Tearing at the leaves of the surrounding jungle with an almost deadly force. However, the palms and lesser foliage were not intimidated. They simply shook their heads in angry compliance with the wind and absorbed the storms strength, directing the water toward the ground where it could be properly dealt with. The jungle floor's thin soil would divide the nutrients and minerals feeding the trees and undergrowth in payment for their protection. All here was reasoned and balanced. All here was absorbed and used. Survival was bound to the old Spanish phrase " What can not be changed must be endured." Nature ruled here.

In the house with its heavy polished wood doors and bulletproof windows, no one ruled. Perhaps, I might have, had I the soul left, had I not been a husk, a hulk tormented by the searing pain of loss. Michael McFurson widower. It sounded old fashioned and conjured white hair, rocking chairs and a momentary last breath.

As the Dutch say 'too early old and too late smart.' A man to his sorrow becomes comfortable with the other half of his half. His wife is lost in the day to day. The security of his mates presence. Her soft features, the warmth of her body, her ready strength in the daily struggles as they come, is a hammered and tested guarantee. A simple earth assuring hug that metals the spine and enfolds the heart.

Grief is encased in, "I should have done, kissed, touched, listened, cared more about her, then the all powerful center of my universe, me!

I have dragged my pitying dregs across the Gulf of Mexico from the Turks Islands to this desolate spot. Resigned my position, taken my pension from Her Majesty's Secret Service, given grudgely by the new masters and come here to this fast fortress of the mind. To do what? Die perhaps?

No! to heal away from the things that remind me of her. To escape her scent and her clothing, places where she still stood by the door or by the dresser, in my mind, my children and the funeral in that order. God help me, but that organized, over priced pain feast was bad. They tell me it takes two years to grieve the loss of a close relative. What is the computerized estimate for a wife and companion.

At the moment I , Michael D'Iverville McFurson lay in my hammock, fortified in my self pity, looking down the tree lined trail from the main Gulf road bordering the sea. The waves roar up the beach powered by my anger at everything. Yet they calm me. The sea has always calmed me. That and God to whom I have maintained a life long attachment. My faith in the fact that my wife is with him and waiting for me somehow balances out the new me that has emerged. As a professional spy and someone who has taken life, perhaps it is easier. There are so many whom I have closed a file on. That's not right! Seen into a better place? To hell with it, seen dead! I hope there is a better place . At first I thought her death was associated with my other life in payment for long ago sins. A thorough investigation found that death had come on the wheels of a five ton lorry with bad brakes. This vehicle, the property of a poor man, who did not have the money to repair them and support his six children. Lothfull poverty, grinding everything and everyone to make do and to have a little more then nothing. The man cried for his state and his make do sin and I in the end comforted him.

Here, the hacienda, the former fortress of a friendly Firm, provided a monk's solitude to soften the blow allowed me to slowly escape the black aloneness, allowed me to think again. The strength had come back, the needs, the reality of survival and life. I know now I have more of the jungle in me than I had suspected. Her features are harder to remember even after a short time. Am I so callused that I have no sense of mortal loss. Has the life I have lived robbed me, made me a void, made me cold and unresponsive to the one thing in my life that should have meaning.

The woman moves about at the other end of the long cool hallway in the kitchen and then purposely into another room. She works constantly thinking nothing of it. It is her responsibility and her livelyhood. My fortress secures her life and that of her moppet. Insures she eats and lives in a clean environment. The village is a puss ridden study of rural poverty. She would find no work and be a prostitute there, from need, not desire. This native beauty might have followed that path, before Torro the last owner found her perfect, petite body to his liking and brought her here to survive with him.

The woman's movements are subdued and quiet as if sensing my thoughts focusing on her. She is out of view much of the time, fearing perhaps I will find fault and banish them to the dark poverty outside. I like to think it is to protect my sad thoughts from outward stimulus.

You do not hear the child. Although I sense her small presence playing or writing or drawing.. Trained to silence so that the Patron will not be disturbed. Learned over the years, at six she is almost perfect. Periodically there is whimpered protest over bed or other matters but these are quickly stilled.

The woman brings lemon juice and places the glass on the table next to me. Her silent movements punctuated by the soft pat of her bare feet on the hardwood floor and the now familiar scent of her body. My nose searches for its unique mixture, insurance of her presence. My sense glands rewarded with the proximity of floor wax, polish, spicy food and her own earthy but clean body odor. This scent like the jungle, part of the nature of the place. I glance up and she smiles an embarrassed flush. Was she looking at me fondly? She is beautifully formed, small in size as are most of her people. Her compact body is covered with the copper skin of a Central American native but her face is semi-Caucasian. The soulful, bottomless brown eyes of her heritage, surrounded with a heart like European face coming toa soft point at the chin. She shyly flashes a second friendly smile uncovering flawless white teeth beneath a turned up almost Irish nose. Jet black hair comes down to her neck. Her body is full. The hips move with their own slow Latin rhythm as she retreats to the kitchen. Confidence has grown only slightly in her from that first awkward day.

I had seen the house and the price had been agreed upon . The representative of His Holy

Roman Catholic Majesty's Secret Service had led me down the hall for one last look. The Woman appeared as if by magic in a corner by the door of her room. The Moppet in a wide yellow dress stood before her pressing against her mother for protection. The child's great wide eyes watched as fate walk toward them. The Woman stood there straight, tensed between flight and assault, shielded by a bravery, which was as brittle as the crust of spring snow. A chance for her and her child. Maybe if the Gringo had no one then she might have a chance. What prayer had been said? What promises to her God had been made, just to stay? What would she do if there is no place for her? That reality is forgotten, only bravery now. Vasques the Spaniard was perturbed probably having told her to disappear before my coming.

"She worked here for Torro." He said with a flick of his fingers like he might be removing something vile from them.

" Does she live in?" I asked

" For Toro yes, for you? I think yes." He smiled a leer. I nodded

" Ask her if she will stay on and be the maid for five dollars more a week." I suggest.

"You can have her for much less." The Spaniard protested. The woman's eyes flashed from one face to the other knowing her fate and that of her child was being decided, unable to understand the language. She was living on the fear of returning to the poverty of the village which one could smell outside if the wind was blowing the wrong way.

"Ask her!" I say firmly. He does as I command.

" Si, Si Gracious Senior." She smiles. Her eyes are bright. I smile back reassuringly.

" She must go to the doctor. I will pay, and for the child too." I finish,

" Caution !This is very smart." Says the diplomat come realtor.

In truth had she not been in the house I would have gone mad. The aloneness would have destroyed me. Not in itself but the longing for what is past and cannot be had again  would have been more then I could handle.

The sun room, come screened porch I sit in, has been painfully built by local labour with a lot of yelling and many mistakes it gets done. This addition extends my view laterally beyond the great rock which blocks the house from the sea and its consistent ferocity.

I need to see the waves. The ever present living sea, calm and blue or gray and oily as today. I can watch it forever. It is my lover, my food and my drink, it dulls the pain, gives me the lassitude of far away. Day dreams of my lost love.

The Saab turns up our pothole drive as if it is destined. After seeing the same view for so long, placid in its sameness, the new Saab seems surreal. The Saab splashes up under the car port immediately below me, so that I must stand to see my immaculately dressed visitor step out of his expensive set of Swedish wheels.

## Chapter two - 9:45 McFurson's Castle, San Terriora El Terra, Central America

The Pitch

The Spaniard and he could be nothing else stood at the door. Not simply Latin or local or even local with bloodlines that dated back to Ferdinand and Isabella, but a Spaniard with a wardrobe purchased in Madrid only weeks before. He must be Torro's replacement, although I had been assured he would be situated in the capital. His appearance here should raise some alarm bells and strangely they did ring. It seemed my survival instinct was alive and well.

The Don was tall perhaps six feet and well proportioned with a large squarish Catalonian face. His large hands were involved in the endeavor of popping his knuckles while bright, questioning, brown eyes scanned the house. Beneath a full head of curly, jet black hair a short forehead fell to a rather large nose supported by a full mouth and strong chin.

Almost before a knock was heard the Woman was in the door frame requesting with her eyes if this stranger might enter. I nodded.

I moved from the window where the rain pushed

in a cooling breeze, while the overly wide roof removed the inconvenience of becoming wet and met him at the door to my sanctum.

" It is a pleasure to meet you." He said in perfect English while providing me with a toothy grin. Sometimes you like people on sight, this was one.

"Allow me to introduce myself, I am Mahwell De Santa Loirenta." I knew without asking that his name was longer then provided. Intermarriage between the great families of Spain always demanded the addition of excess but important reminders of heritage. This man was truly a Don. His fine features bespoke perhaps even royal blood . The  bearing of his stance was a banner for machismo as only the Spanish upper-class have at their disposal.

I shook his hand and directed him to a small table with two comfortable wooden lawn chairs flanking it.

" I am Michael McFurson but then you'll know that." I said with an equally toothy grin. He laughed in a deep honest baritone and nodded.

" Torro thought highly of you." He said by way of a complement. In my time I had gotten to know most of the denizens of the World as we called the spy game in the Caribbean and surrounding areas. I had even had the pleasure of working with Torro

briefly. He was a good man, big as a buffalo and
strong as an elephant. A bald dome, large pirate like
beard and a laugh to wake the dead. He had left this
world at the age of thirty-eight of a heart attack.
Want to buy some swamp land cheap? The
Spaniards didn't believe it either and were looking
into the matter. Perhaps that was what had brought
my visitor so far from the  pleasures of the capital.

   " I wish to apologize for coming here
unannounced." His hands spread to show he is
powerless over the matter. So it was business and in
my retirement years too, nasty, nasty.

   " I am retired as you know and completely
severed from any outside attachments." I said. But
he held up his hand as if I need not warn him off.
As I had come to the point and while he would have
rather  taken his time getting around to the topic he
cut to the chase

   " The matter I have come on has little to do with
you personally, it involves a situation which has
been brought to our attention and may be a source
of positive return for both our companies." He
ended. Creative, positive word development was a
dead giveaway for some really ugly problem that
had to be solved soon.  The fact that my friend had
appeared here might mean big trouble for yours

truly which I did not want and could not really handle at this point.

" I am sure someone at our consulate would be able to help if it involves the government." I said not rudely but that could come later. I didn't want to play.

" No! My reason for coming here is because  you are out of the way, so to speak. The matter is of the strictest confidence and requires delicate handling."

" A secret told is not a secret." I said getting closer to rude.

"True. But in this case we have no other choice. If you listen I will explain." He seemed sincere.

" No! I could not help you and secrets can have nasty effects on your heath. Take Torro for instance." If that didn't work I had lots more. He hesitated only a moment. Then started.

" There is a listening post up the coast in a neighboring country. The post is very high technology and can hear things in Florida as well as around the entire gulf. As you can understand with the American head quarters for the expected difficulties in the Middle East being in Florida this is most unfortunate." That was news. Very important news.  I had to follow up now, damn it, but slowly with as little exposure for me as possible because this could be a trap and everything had to be right.

" If you tell the Americans they will take care of your problem in about ten minutes.' I said bluntly 'Also seeing your one of their biggest allies in this little Middle Eastern thing it would be a feather in your cap too." This stank to high heavens and I wasn't making any commitments.

" Ah! Yes! The Americans." He said like I had reminded him his fly was open. He had a habit of tensing his face like he had just smelled effluent when he was uncomfortable. Mahwell's face twitched that way now as he leaned forward like someone might hear. Oh goody! I look out the window thinking how far off shore a ship had to be to listen in? The Americans could probably hear us from the Keys without too much trouble. Satellites also passed my mind. The problem was I was in now so I played the game.

" The difficulty is that the Americans tend to stay." Mahwell said as politely as possible. I sat back in my chair and evaluated this new perspective. The Americans had been in most all of these little countries like a shuttlecock over the years. Removing regimes, reorganizing standing governments, everybody down here was overjoyed with American reorganization. As a matter of fact word was they were building trade blocks to counter that nation The fact the listening post existed would be found suspect  The host country probably didn't have the organization to know what was going on in the next street let alone in some out of the way spot, however, it would still be held responsible. Your government has an excellent marine corps who could clean this thing up  without too much trouble. They did well with the Moroccans." He smiled at that little jab but not much.

" Unfortunately, they left before we could give them the party we arranged." His smile got nasty and mine got sheepish. He continued. " We could take care of this matter, unfortunately we have a very delicate role here  in the Latin American countries. We offer a voice for smaller countries. A voice which, sometimes conflicts with that of the United States. We do not want to increase our involvement here any more then necessary as you can understand." On consideration he was right, armed force used here would be against the Monroe Doctrine and the Don's had been bad guys since the Spanish American War in the American's view.

" Your Country on the other hand has territories in the Caribbean. This listening post would be a threat. Also your contribution to the unpleasantness in the Middle East will be larger then ours. It would be understandable if you protected your people." he finished feeling confident he had achieved his goal.

" I'm a Canadian, my country isn't even going to be in the unpleasantness and for good reason. This may be the only time I have ever agreed with our Prime Minister on anything. However, Regime Change is what your friends down here are afraid of. " He tried to interrupt but I cut him off. " I understand about terrorists. I don't think 1,500 people a month should be tortured and killed and admittedly that is an honorable thing to stop. I guess I would be more receptive if all that lovely crude wasn't involved. The Americans are running out and it's going to take time for them to change over to hydrogen.  Just for the record there are a lot of people around who are worse than the one they're after. You and I know the people who are going to suffer are the poor average shmoes Saddam controls, who don't want the war to begin with and their kids."

" Awh! If you bring down one Dictator the others will be warned. Things may change. If you do nothing no one will change. Also the people you used to work for disagree with you." Mahwell played his one trump card but it didn't pass.

" That in part is why I am retired." I said gruffly. His face fell. " However , I won't see some Royal

Marine or SAS man die because I didn't do my job.
There are lots of Canadians in the British forces as
well I'd like them to come home too. So tell me the
situation and I will do what I can." I sat back to
listen.

" The installation is in an ancient Myna City
Imtuepostichec. We feel a small group of men
could remove the threat. However, the installation
is guarded by about one hundred and fifty
mercenaries."

" And the Americans missed this how ? They
have satellites that can tell you how much lint there
is in your belly button and pick up a light bulb from
five miles up." I asked exasperated.

" Myna ruins are mainly stone. The majority of
the site is underground. The electrical components
are protected from detection. Also the Americans
are not looking for this place. In World War Two
American bombers flew over the death camps took
pictures but they were looking for factories the
labor areas were unimportant. so they saw nothing
of importance." Mahwell stopped for a minute then
continued. " Also We had some luck. A shepherd
lost some goats. "

" You've got to be kidding!" Mahwell laughed at
my astonishment.

" No! Goats! He could not find them and slept out near the temple. In the morning he heard the mechanics of the place operating. From a vantage point he watched them open the dish they use. He walks to the nearest police station. Being a poor man he thinks his information is worth something. Fortunately, one of the senior police officers was on an inspection tour. He spoke to the shepherd realized what it was and brought him back to the capital where he is now in a part of the Presidential Palace. Only the President, our ambassador and a very few  government people know aside of you and I ." Mahwell finished.

" What is the time frame." I asked. These little nation's security were traditionally trained and controlled by the US. They were for the most part a secret in a sieve. However, should something really important and internal come up they can be quiet as the grave.

" A week or two, no more." Mahwell returned, That could mean everyone knew.

" Who are the opposition?" I asked having a pretty good idea to start with.

" We don't know for sure. However, there is Panama." Mahwell threw off . Yes there was the peoples Republic with their huge investment in the old canal. The Russians might finance something like this. For that matter the Germans or the French. Knowledge was power after all.

" These mercenaries what are we looking at." I probed again.

" Some local, some foreign, Cuban officers." Manwell concentrated on the table.

" Ah!' I said ,.Cubans meant well organized tough opposition .' The Cigar isn't behind this? " I asked.

" No! Too much investment." Said the Spaniard, This is very technical, very concentrated the entire operation was brought in on one mule train. All the construction was completed by the people on sight."

" These ancient temples are big money for the locals how come the Cubans aren't  up to their behinds in tourists?"

" The location is very far out, up a mountain. No roads go in. It would cost a fortune to develop. That money does not exist here."

" So you want it disposed of?' Mahwell nodded. ' And we get in addition to your undying love." I bring the matter to a head.

" As you know we have a very good source base in South America and Central America much better than yours for a number of reasons including cost.

We would be willing to let you have  three months
of that information."

" Six!" I said immediately.

" Three and our undying love."

" Your talking taking out bunkers. And maybe
world war three. Six!"

" Four and our undying love. I can go no higher."
And that children is how deals are made.

## Chapter Three - 9:45 Am , Her Majesty's Secret Service Headquarters, London,

The Temerity of it all!

Turner gripped the base of the window frame with vice like fingers. His whip hard body tensed from the hands to his toes stretching upward until he stood on the points of his shoes. He then let go with a deep, windy sigh dropping back to the floor. One would think Turner had completed a circus trick as his arms crossed on this chest coming to a standing position. Peaches thought the selection of body movements looked remarkably like a moving picture of Hitler in his youth. There was little resemblance between the two men but Peaches choose the image as he didn't like the new head of shop very much and his seniority with the Firm allowed him a little self gratifying arrogance.

Turner, the spy master, as he might fancy himself in the hierarchy of the world, turned from the window abruptly and prowled toward his highly polished cherry wood desk it seemed with the intention of attacking it. The step was aggressive for a frame which was small but powerful. A no nonsense man for a no nonsense time. In control , well, as in control as might be possible, in a world where weapons of mass destruction  appeared and disappeared with regularity and then seemed to vanish all together. How could one control  matters down the hall? However, Turner gave a roaring good mime of doing just that.

The new spy chief's hard, almost brittle, gray eyes came up off the desk to look through Edward Ascot Peaches who sat opposite. Peaches surveyed Turner's countenance with a neutral interest. The gob beneath a brownish wig, which fitted reasonably well, displayed a short rectangular forehead, pencil thin eyebrows and a small sharp nose. That almost straight line added what little charm there was to Turner's angular flinty face, with its tight little mouth. The Spy Master had martinet written all over him.

Peaches sat cross legged with his body completely at rest. One of the oldest denizens of the Firm's Head Office he had something on everyone and was not to be trifled with. Completely loyal but not strong enough to lead, Peaches or Peachy as everyone called him was an excellent support person, a fine sounding board and a veritable encyclopedia of information on all facets of the organization. He might have been Philby but he was not that kind of man.

Peachy was a portrait of clandestine efficiency in contrast to the newest resident of the great corner office overlooking the river. Kind brown eyes twinkled with life, gently removing years from his sixty something body with it's pear shape and balding plate. Peachy reeked of good tailoring , good breeding and good fun. Nothing could phase the gentle slope of his face which, was hyphenated by a smiling mouth and friendly devil be damned ease of place. One would be hard pressed to choose two men more opposite in disposition or personality. Yet by some miracle of brinkmanship the duet worked together like well oiled components of a high tech machine.

Peachy places his four finger vertically across his lips leaving a fingerprint on his upper lip. This was an indication of lack of interest and a need to move on. Turner spotted it immediately and turned away to begin speaking as if he feared the older man would read his thoughts.

" Bloody McFurson, every able bodied line agent I have is doing a Lawrence of Arabia, in support of a probable war, the Irish coming apart and now listening posts on the Central American Coast." He let his hands fall in exasperation. " What am I to do with this lot?" He finished angrily.

" Perhaps we should look at the situation as an opportunity to get all that lovely information from the Dons. It's certainly a coup. We could confirm a lot of our own stuff get some good leads. The potential on an industrial level is enormous and if I might point out old darling a once in a life time portal." Peachy finished a little less formally then he usually did but Turner was in such a quandary he did not take offence. At heart the Spy Master was never sure of what he was doing unless he had done it before. Of course, if you could direct him to the target, he would move heaven and earth to reach it. There should have been action on this Spanish thing two days ago but they were still sniffing at it. Madrid must  wonder what the hell was going on? The question had certainly occurred to him. Turner swiveled and gave the venerable Peaches a look that would curdle milk. He didn't like the old boy in house, incivility that went with Eaton and  the like. It sounded nancy boy and sod like. Turner appreciated neither.

" And who the hell do I bloody send? ' He asks hand on hip.' Ever do over a bunker?' Peachy looked down and away it was obvious he had not. 'I did in the Falklands it's not as easy as you might think." Old memories surrounded the Spy Master for a moment and Peaches being sensitive to the situation and his own well being said nothing.

" The Middle East has all our specialists at the moment, Marines, Commando's the lot. I couldn't pry a seeing eye dog and a mess cook out of the Army to save my life, let a lone an assault force . The Navy if anything is in worse shape. All our own people are spoken for. Perhaps we should tell the Yanks?" He said as if giving up.

" That certainly isn't cricket after all the Don's came to us in confidence. Surely we have someone in the Caribbean . Bermuda must have a unit or other laying about?" Peaches admonished. The Spy Master shook his head.

" Picked clean I'm afraid."

" Our chap in Nassau is good." Peaches made a lukewarm attempt.

" Our Caribbean stations are a great flaming disaster. The greatest concentration of slackers and scrum shakers on record. Half the information we get is old or unusable, most of them are retirement age and the few good ones I can't waste on some death trap like this." Then as if the Head of Station had been hit by a sledge the answer was there.

"Oh God!" Said Peachy under his breath sensing the cold blooded calculation going on beneath the rug.

" Contact. Fish, Sanders, Let me see. Oh Yes!
Bloody McFurson. He found this little fiddle he'll
make a jolly good lead for the expedition. Also that
worthless sotted prat Mason, the so called explosive
expert and Lorning he's been buggering around the
Caymans far too long. Yes! Brilliant! If they bugger
it up the Yanks will find out and we've done our
best. The Yanks will take care of it. Our pension list
will be down  and the Spaniards will be required to
pay up. If they do pull it off we take the credit, the
information and look like heroes." The head of
station was jolly proud of himself. Peaches anger
was tangible but of course it was the only way. It
would leave room for a number of the Spy Masters
friends and probably relatives to go out  and give
their all in the warm Caribbean sunshine. On the
other hand the idea had real problems and he must
point them out.

" You realize of course you're talking a mountain
covered in jungle. Fish must be 30 stone he'd have
a heart attack. Half the others are as old or worse.
We are talking dense jungle sixty miles from the
nearest road . How are you going to get them there
rappel down from a helicopter?"

"Are you mad on my budget. No! Land Rovers
will do nicely. They can be looking for birds or
butterflies or something. I'll work it out with

Ridley. The bloody mountain is their problem."
Turner sneered to a stop.

" They might resign." Peachy pointed out.

"Let them! " Said the Spy Master as if it might
have been part of the original plan.

" McFurson is retired."

"We'll resurrect him. He was the one who came
up with this lot." Snarled Turner.

" He has a resignation document you know."
Peaches said with a slightly triumphant smile.

" He has a what?' The Spy Master turned around
with a comic look of horror on his face that might
have reflected blasphemy on the part of Peaches.
'You're mad no one gets a document."

" Brae signed one for him, cheeky lad." Peaches
was enjoying the slight purple shade of the Spy
Masters face.

" Is it legal?" Demanded the thunderstruck
Turner.

" Oh Rather! I drew it up myself.' Peaches
confirmed. 'He could take us to court you know."
Peachy threw that one out just to see what would
happen. The Spy Master swallowed audibly, all that
nasty publicity . Peaches could see visions of the
case in Canada coming to Turners mind where one

of their part timers had taken CISIS to small claims Court and spilled the beans so to speak. Leaving a red faced lawyer from that venerable spy Firm blathering national secrets act after every statement. A lot of juicy stuff about extra rooms being added to senior employees homes with government money. What a farce!

" He wouldn't dare." said the shaken Turner.

" He might if pushed he just lost his wife you know?" Peachy put in.

"Mean he's unstable maybe a Section 5" Turner was considering putting down McFurson like a lame old dog.

" I shouldn't think so he does hold the VC you know. There might well be questions from the palace down." Peachy said softly.

" And they would become aware of it how?" Turner was very cold now.

" There are parts of our government where you are not well loved." Peachy countered. Turner had a way of turning people on himself.

" Yes! They would too, wouldn't they?" For a moment he considered the situation. Then there was a spark, the voice became more amiable perhaps even considerate.

" McFurson will go because he's Queen and country. He's honorable, his conscience will make him. The others will do as they are bloody well told. Send the e-mails. Have them meet me in San Juan, Puerto Rico. Peachy see that the meeting room at the hotel is checked for sounders and such and send someone out to cover me." With this the Spy Master left for Ridley's office.

Chapter Four - 2:10 Am, Central American Coast, McFurson's Castle

Sparkles On The Water

I considered Turners message and weighted it's significance against everything that surrounded me and brought me joy. Slowly my depression come loneliness was becoming less and less. I enjoyed the house, reveling in it's solitude. I had time, time to read a book or sleep as I willed and relax. Really relax not napping with one eye open so to speak.

Turner wanted me to return to his world of creeping paranoia, clandestine meetings with people you wouldn't want to know in real life. To do what? To save the lives of people who would never know you had done it thousands of miles away.

At the moment I was immersed in something very special so I gave Turner the toss for tonight and concentrated on something I though I had forgotten. Sex!.

The woman in question stood against the metal railing of the veranda that overlooked my faded blue pool deck and scrupulous clean if small kidney shaped pool. I should mention she was a surprise and a pleasant one. A jazz singer tall and blond.

However, everything about her was out of
proportion. Out of a dress and with her hair pinned
up in a bun. She had a body that became a
delightful selection of oddities. At the moment her
feet were in open backed  clogs. Resting her weight
against the railing, she lifted first one ankle then the
other so the white soul showed. Beyond that she had
a deep honey colored tan that covered every visible
part of her. Her legs perfectly shaped and
magnificent seemed to rise forever in lightly
muscled splendor until they hit the stop sign that
was her bottom. It was as if a lolly pop had grown
there. The hips were wide and firm but her behind
was nonexistent. This pitifully flat area was
presently covered by jean cutoffs so old and
weathered that it seemed they were held together
with the patches added to offer greater cover. The
cloth had worn through showing enticing strips of
white skin as she rocked from one foot to the other.
She was either wearing a thong.  I consider The
Camel's toe as some girls define it a foolish piece
of sexual apparel. Either you show it or you don't.
On the other hand she might be wearing nothing at
all. I would give you odds on the latter.
   My Jazz lady was just that type. There is
something uniquely sexual about having a woman

doggy style, who is deeply tanned but whose bottom is a pure expanse of white skin.

A thirty-two inch waist is perfect but on my Jazz singer it just accentuated the "V" of her back and her wide almost muscular shoulders. She wore a frilly blue sleeveless half shirt  that tied in the front under small if appealing breasts. Without the cascade of golden blond hair her neck seemed stem like, resembling  a pool Q, holding up a number three ball. The head which now turned into my gaze was too small for her frame. Yet with all these negatives, there was something tremulously sexual about her and alluring. She was like  a perfume your senses catch in a moment and are intoxicated by. You desperately strain to keep the moment  but it is gone.

Was it the knowing face with its quick green-gray eyes, small delicate nose and purse like mouth that enraptured you? More than likely it was the way her fine long fingers ran down  her thighs periodically, reminding her audience of the potential of who and what she was.

"You were good tonight " she said off handedly as one professional would to another rather than someone giving a complement which was required.

I play the piano badly. I play it in my bar. The makeshift cantina comes with the house. Originally

in another incarnation the bar was a Petra Fina
Station. It now sported a single garage. This was
run by Thomas a lean, wiry Honduran who could
repair anything on wheels and had to, given we
were the only petrol station for miles.

The remainder of the building including the big
glassed in service area where tires and oil had once
been  displayed was now a bar with a few tables and
chairs. The cantina sold mainly cheep local beer to
the fishermen and better stuff to the few moneyed
people who dropped in. In this area it was Spanish
beat music that held the crowd but the Steinway
Baby grand that forced the tables outside onto the
patio was too good a chance to miss. So one or two
nights a week I would play all my old favorites
usually slow elevator type stuff. The crowd seemed
to like the change at least they didn't come at me.
Anyway I was the heffey and Mariano the barkeep
took orders from me. The Spanish like my own
secret service made sure their outposts paid for
themselves. Torro had taken advantage of the fact
selling beer to the fishermen at night and gas for
their boats in the morning.

Shylow McCormick the Jazz lady had sent out a
letter to all the reasonably sized cantina's  in the
area and I thought it might be nice to back her up on
the ivories . I guess I expected someone more like

me. The singer would be older, about the end of her
tether maybe a drunk or on drugs. I figured I make
the decision when I saw her. If she was really bad
I'd just pay her and send her on her way. Part of the
deal was a place for the night. There weren't any
hotels so it was my castle in the  guest  room or
nothing

When Shylow arrived she was all business from
the get go. The Jazz Lady was exactly as advertised
and was treated  that way too so no passes from
anyone.  That night  half the Province showed up. I
did a little advertising of my own. The beer sales
were brisk and the music at least the singing was
pure heaven. It came from deep inside her. Blues
based on the shear joy of being. The entertainment
starved crowd was enraptured as the golden hair
swung around her face and the songs touched the
soul. Shylow got three standing ovations and we ran
out of suds, tequila and just about everything else.
After close up she and I jammed for a while doing
things with the music. I tried to keep up but she was
way out of my class. Finally at two in the morning
we ended up here. Me sitting on one of my over
padded lawn chairs, she leaning against the railing
of my patio.

It was hot but the wind off the Gulf found us and played with her hair offering a little restpite.

" Shylow that's different." I said to make conversation. Her laughter was rich and velvety like the night. The Jazz Lady could have been twenty or thirty it didn't matter odds on she was older

" My father liked the song but he wasn't much of a speller." She confided.

" You are really good. Why sing down here? Why not up north where the money is better and you don't have to worry about being shot at among other things." I asked a little dumfounded.

" What's a nice girl like you doing in a place like this?" She countered with a laugh.

" Did it sound like that? Sorry!"

"Don't be. " she shook her head to the negative. 'I was up there but I like it down here. Big fish, little pond. I don't usually do places this small and I wasn't real sure about this staying at your house."

" There is a room behind the cantina." I offered.

" No! I think I'll stay here. It's a really nice place." another compliment she seemed tired and I was about to suggest she go to bed. When she changed the subject.

"What's a nice man like you doing in a place like this?" She asked. Sometimes the truth comes out when it's too late at night and you feel a lot of things you shouldn't.

"Vegetating, I lost my wife and came here to die I guess. Now it's not as bad and I get this horrible feeling I'm going to survive and that really scares me." I finished as she laughed.

" There is definitely a song in there somewhere.' She teased. 'Seeing you're being so honest I have a question."

"Shoot!" I said with a grandiose wave of my arms.

" Did you hire me thinking you'd screw me?" I was a little taken aback because I had not pushed it. One trick I learned long ago is, if a woman asks you if you want to have sex with her? Always tell the truth. If you tell her its her mind your after she knows you're a damned liar anyway.

" Yes! I'm a semi-sane, heterosexual, adult male of course I would like to have sex with you. Hell! If you went into heat or something there would be a line up back to Mexico City of men wanting to have sex with you." Now she really laughed. Finally she stopped looked at me hard for a moment, you could see a decision had been made.

" I want to go swimming you mind?" She asked.

" Sure, I'll swim with you," I said without thinking.

" Sure !" her smile was knowing. Then she kicked off her clogs , untied her blouse and presented me with two silken mounds that might just fill your hand. Her dark nipples were hard in the dim light of the pool.

" They're beautiful " I said rising from my chair. Shylow said nothing but her smile became kinder . I could hear the metallic slide of her zipper on its way down. My gaze came up from dropping my bathing suit to see her standing waiting . A six pack rippled above her mons which was as golden as her mane. She turned without speaking and walked slowly toward the steps that lead down to the pool. The gentle undulations of her bottom transfixed my view and I followed like a puppy. Perhaps it was the night  or the heat or the fact that we were the only two white North Americans in a hundred miles? In life something's just work out right all the weights and balances are equal. I knew we would sleep together it was an unstated fact as perfect as the moment. My body reacted badly as it must.

The water was warm as a bath tub she swam slowly letting the shimmering dots of light slide over her. I swam a little too but my body ached for her. Finally she came over and pressed her stomach to mine. We kissed then. She lifted herself and slowly settled on to me. The strength of the love making first in the pool and later in her bed feeling her ankles against the back of my neck was so powerful Every **muscle** in my body strained to get deeper, closer, more totally a part of her. Low moans breathed in my ear drove me on and on until I trembled with the force of my finish and hers. It is not often you share the explosion together and the wonderful aftermath.

In the morning she had breakfast, then left with a smile and a wave. I missed her and hoped she would return but I knew in my soul I would never see her again. In her wake though she left me more alive then I had been in months. She had in her gentle musicians way given me back my manhood with no strings attached. I was now ready to face Turner.

Chapter Five - 10:25 Pm The Cantina, McFurson's
Castle, The Gulf Coast, Central America

A Little Bird

 The fishermen had sailed long ago with the rising
sun to harvest the local waters. There were few
large boats. Yet these strong decent men in their
ragged clothing, with wheezing motors, old canvas
and hands callused by a life time of pitiless work
went out each day to face a merciless sea. Each day
they ventured forth with a fresh buoyant attitude as
enduring as the sun which  made there bodies rich
mahogany brown .
 The children had left early as well. It seems
someone had purchased a case of shoes and got
some books sent down from the capital. There were
shirts , shorts and dresses traded for fresh fish.  To
the fishermen this was a blessing of unique almost
priceless objects. The classes at the church run
school had doubled. In this land of little a better
future depended on extravagances like shoes, a new
shirt, a copy book and a pencil those who had these
things could learn. The fishermen knew what I had
done and they would remember. Little things have
value if they are done properly. I now had fast

friends and a freezer overflowing with fish.

The woman's Moppet joined the packed school. I paid for her. This was also appreciated.

The woman and I had started out poorly . On the first night at the house after my high blood pressure pill and a quiet drink, I was off to dream land. I awoke quivering at the soft pat of a bare feet which brought me around fast. The Kalibur IPSC 357 Magnum , hidden under my pillow, centered its five inch barrel  on the nude body of my maid come house keeper caught in the light like a small animal in the high beams of a car. As soon as I recognized her I placed the weapon on the bed noting that the rubber grip was moist with sweat. She made no sound. The Canadian made magnum seemed to fascinate her like a snake might a sparrow. I on the other hand had a moment to enjoy the view which was magnificent. Her breasts were full and large, ample dark brown nipples were presented without modesty. The coffee coloured waist was perfectly formed providing a heart shape background for her mons vagina which stood out forcefully beneath a pillow like tummy. She had short but finally shaped legs and small delicate feet with small short toes.

I should be ready to accept the offering but could not. First, because it was too close to my wife's death. Secondly, I felt shame at her simple acceptance of being house whore to support her child. That reality was unacceptable to the nth degree.

"You are very beautiful,' I said choosing my words carefully in Spanish which I speak rather well but this was important. 'You are not required to sleep with me. Your position is secure. Only do your job well and I request nothing more." She looked a little afraid she had offended. God how could we have so much and they so little. 'My wife has just died and it is much too soon for me. You did not know. Do not be distressed, your gift is a wonderful one and if things were different then I would accept it gratefully."

" I am sorry" she started.

" You have nothing to apologize for. Go to bed."

" Si Patron " she whispered and left showing me a wonderful saddled bottom. I was tempted to call her back, but no! When you play by the rules all your life then you stick with it.

" I was pleased with my decision. The moppet and I got to know each other better. While her mother worked the little one would come and sit behind my chair to watch the television. I would talk to her and she would tell me about her day and its important events. After a while I would leave the set on playing cartoons for her when I went off to do other things. This was appreciated too and not forgotten by her mother.

At the moment I was involved with making sure my gas delivery was correct. There was always an extra price. A pay off and of course a long conversation about everything. I dealt honestly with honest men where I could, other times you just took it. I had just seen the back of the greasy crook who was my fuel distributor when the BMW roared up. Regal in it's cover of dust it stopped by the pumps and ejected a medium size very blond German and his medium size very blond wife who started to take pictures of the boats and the shore line. I noted she was meticulous in not shooting the cantina or the house. Both of my guests were  immaculately dressed in perfect tourist togs and of course were Firm people. How do you know? Well! They were trying too hard for a start. Another point was that the man came in directly to me like a homing pigeon, smiling like I was a long lost brother. He was probably happy to find me without having to spend hours searching. The Deucher didn't seem to be a threat or armed. Although Mariano's hand rested on a greener he kept behind the bar. As manager he depended on me for a living so the German was liable to get blown in half if anything funny happened. The man in gray golf shirt was about five foot eleven, with a sharp Nordic face, strong cheek bones, a delicate nose and slash mouth. His eyes  were a cynical, pasty blue if that was possible?

" Could you have them put petrol in my car please?" He said in immaculate English. It might be that he was figuring I was an American or he knew exactly what he was dealing with., I bet on the latter.

" Is there a place of privacy where we might talk?" He asked politely there is no name given but I don't expect one.

" Your standing in it." My reply was a little blunt but then I'm retired and don't need this crap.

" Of course." He smiles showing perfect teeth. The value of the capping alone would feed the village for six months. He looks at his Rolex as if considering if he was on time then begins.

" You are Herr McFurson, yes? " he asks just to get it right.

"And if I were?" I say playing the game but badly.

" I have a message from my head office for you.' He accepts I am the target of his visit. 'You see this house of yours has a history which you might not know and may be important to you."

" Really!" I am not enthusiastic having visions of having to move just when I have the place where I want it.

" The house you know was built in the late fifties.
There are some who might suggest ODESSA money
was spent here. One thing is certain A Herr Roln
Starvinggant. lived here at that time. He held the rank
Assistant Commandant at one of the camps. We of
course kept a file on him and the house. The Israelis
tried to arrest Roln here but he escaped. Later he died
in Argentina of what might be considered natural
causes. The house has had quite a few owners we
kept an eye on it because of the ODESSA  {ODESSA
just for the unanointed is the organization set up after
World War II  to get Nazis war criminals out of
Germany) tie in but that seemed to end with
Starvinggant.

However, in the seventies just before the fall of
Pol Pot. A certain General Tow Kei was one of the
men in power during the time of  the killing fields.
As you know all the cities in Cambodia were
cleared of people most didn't come back."

" They murdered one point seven million ." I threw
in just to tell him I understood.

" Yes.!" He said " appalling." He meant it too ,
"So " I cosed

" General Kei, a Hercules transport and eight huge
weapons crates along with some of
his most trusted body guards left the capital a few

hours before the Vietnamese  arrived
to stop the killing and of course depose Pot who
had been foolish enough to attack them.
  " And Kei effects me how?" I asked.
  " The boxes could have held weapons to be sold
later or perhaps something else. Let us
  say loot. Shall we? "
  " Gold teeth perhaps ?" I ask nastily
  " Yes! Among other things.' he answers angrily .'
Billions in Gold, jewels currency. The
wealth of a dead people. I find it strange and
revolting that the world would allow that kind
of holocaust to occur twice in the same century."
He means this too and I feel a little sorry
for him. His accent is a chain to events he wasn't
old enough to have participate in. It must
be truly strange to have to be ashamed on
command.
History! We live with it I guess.
However, the story was getting interesting so I
pushed a little.
  " And this effects me how?"
  " The plane stopped in Switzerland but the Swiss
wouldn't have it there." He said smiling
  "You've got to be kidding?"
  "No! The question of just how much money was
in all those uncollected Jewish accounts

was  just gaining momentum then and the
gnomes of  Zurich didn't want more bad
publicity. We of course would have nothing to do
with it. Kei did make one stop though
Montreal. The Hercules was sold to a reputable
cargo carrier. The boxes , General Kei
and his associates disappeared ' The Germans
Right  hand closed ' and poof he was here
with his entourage." The left hand opened.
  " The Boxes " I asked a little frightened now to
know.
  " I have no idea. Kei on the other hand tried to
reunite with his family who had been
moved to New York. Unfortunately he fell in with
some unpleasant people and died. We
believe he didn't tell the location of the treasure.
He had a bad heart and died at the scene of
his abduction."
  " So everybody who knows thinks the money is
in the house is that the deal?" I said
uncomfortably.
  " Not really the house I can assure you has
been searched thoroughly by past owners
If it was here it would have been found.
However , there is always the possibility there is
a clue, map something, leading to the treasure if
you like. People are still keeping a eye on

the place. Some local thugs, your chief of police who you seem to know well can tell you about them. Two or three people in the underworld and so on and some drug people but for the most part they don't disturb Firm people for obvious reasons. It might be advisable, however, not to use the services of a certain Dr. Sanchez for instance."

" Any particular reason." I queried.

" He was Torro's doctor and Torro had a heart attack." My Blond friend nodded knowingly.

" You figure Sanchez  helped him along because Torro knew something?"

" It's difficult to say."

" The Spanish wouldn't go for that they'd do him like dinner." I said calculating how blue the purity of the sea was Versus the evil we had gotten into.

" Dr. Enrico Sanchez  is a man of many faces shall we say. Here he works with the poor and offers his services to the rich. He is an excellent medical Doctor. What is even more interesting is he has a practice in New York City. It is said he may even have the backing of interested parties in the US"

" My, My doctors write their own ticket in the big apple. Why come back here?"

" You've heard of electronic mental evaluation." He asked.

" Isn't that a deal where they hook the person watching TV with electrodes in a helmet then they read the colours. You can tell if someone is stimulated or not by the colour mix like a mood ring." I venture having heard about on the CBC or somewhere.

" Exactly, of course they have become far more sophisticated now smaller models incursion under the skin. The technical advances amaze and frighten me. They cannot read your mind yet but soon big brother. There was talk that Sanchez went on his own when the American government would not give him suitable test people. Overcharges of electricity used caused madness among other less pleasant things. Strangely there have been some similar cases here. Interesting Nie? The good Herr Doctor is in need of money, the financing for his project has been cut off." he finished

" Is that all." I ask hopping it is

" Yes! "

"And I get this briefing because Berlin is in a good mood today."

" Berlin, I can assure you is never in such a good   mood. ' He smiled. ' It is because,' he became very precise 'Three hundred Germans were able to get off a LufthLiepzig flight alive in New York. We don't forget our friends"

You pay for every good thing you do as the saying goes but sometimes it comes back to you in a different way.

Chapter Six - 9:45 Am, Los Hotel Des Floras, San Juan, Puerto Rico.

Ruminations

The Hotel of Flowers is more the hotel of Oak.. Great rich highly polished pillars of this strong long lasting wood hold up the second story of the hotel. The paneled lobby and the sizable casino whose doors, are never closed gleam with polish.

I sit in the lobby because my hotel room is too depressing. It has all the style of a motel and is so ultramodern, after my time living next to the jungle it scares even me.

Sitting down here is at least interesting. You can people watch. Of course people can also see you but then I'm only here to give a little information then back to jungle and the woman who I am beginning to long for. Perhaps to be honest the little things she does for me draws me to her. She seems to read my mind. Things appear before they are asked for. My drink is always full, my pillow fluffed. Here they are friendly but the service is not the same. I have become pampered and have no shame of it. I need a mother. Now that is a frightening revelation. I find it strange that I yen for my castle. It is quiet there. While the hotel is reasonably tranquil in a well healed way. The traffic outside storms by like a conquering army in a crescendo of victory.

From my seat I can see into the casino, pretty girls in short skirts offer free drinks to the patrons. You know you're not in Ontario. By the door a black jack table is in operation. Five or more players seem to constantly face the suave dark haired mostashiowed dealer. I watch his hands as he deals the cards. Clean simple movements very precise no loose throws or two card drops. The eyes above are watching after all and he is a professional. His fingers are fine and well shaped the moves are pure and tempered. I remember. What do I remember? Yes, of course the book seller. A day or so after the funeral I am dragged off by the kids to at lease walk around and be with people at the local mall. After a few minutes, I excuse myself and let them move along without me. Sitting on a bench and watching the crowd kills the time. The pain was deeper then harder to control. I am about to go to my son's car when I see the book seller. I do not know his name but he is selling books at a signing. Unlike other authors he talks to the people. I realize he has it down to a science. The customer comes up, to the book seller at that point, I calculate he has eight seconds to make his sale. The pitch is simple and the smile genuine. He wears a suit which matches his tie. His hands move the book about. The customer comes closer he flips the book and places it in their hands. Now the pitch slow or fast as required . Each individual is treated like an individual. There is a joke, the book seller laughs the loudest. The pitch completed he now sits back to allow the customer to read the back of the book. Following this the inevitable close. Should the answer be no, he thanks them for their time, if yes he makes a big deal of the sale and signs the book. As a marketer I know he is good but it is his reaction to the customers that is fascinating to watch. He seems to sense where they are and turns. Recognition and the pitch are immediate he is like a big cat in the jungle blending in to it perfectly moving to respond to the prey, closing cleanly. He has the same hands as the dealer. I realize that man must do what is necessary to survive. The book seller making his few dollars per book. The dealer making his salary plus a cut. I being a courier for information. At that moment I would have given anything for my old job. Having value is the trick. It balances everything without it a man is nothing. Many retire and die in a few years because all they are is their job, robbed of it, the position and responsibility it represents. They literally die of displacement. I had the wife she was the center of my universe. The one I could enjoy life with, explore new things like when we were kids. Our children were gone, we were on our own. There was no one else. Now she was gone and I didn't even have my work. It is maudlin to cry in front of strangers so a retreat to my sons car I cried there. I had not cried during the funeral now it was a blessing, it seemed to clear me out. Emptied my emotions allowed me to understand that to survive I must work or at least find a place where I was valued. The castle was that place. My employees, the woman, her child, the fishermen to some extent, the doctor and the boy all required my help. I had transferred the need to protect my family which had been the center of my life and now could take care of itself to protecting and helping these strong but very vulnerable people of the village

Yet each step taken was to strengthen myself and I knew it. The hospital beds I was able to wangle from the Kitchener for free. Beds that were to be thrown out for new ones. Twenty-five of these fit very well into the small hospital the local doctor ran. There was some very basic drugs and some simple basic equipment that saved lives and would have been scrap back home in Canada. Dr. Stephan Alverez the town doctor was immediately at my service and made house calls as I requested. Am I too self centered. Protecting one's behind seems to be a given in this world. If however, you can do it while helping others then you get a much better return on your investment. What is  given back in return is out of want not command or at least I hoped.

The boy! The boy picked himself. No! that is wrong. The donkey and cart that blocked my ancient Rover caused me to pick the boy. At that moment I was situated on the edge of the town dump. There was only one truck delivering and the driver sold his loads of Garbage to the poor starving people who had a centavo. Others who had none waited for the scraps. No! We are not in Kansas any more pokey.  From the window I could follow the movement of the sifters looking for anything to sell from the better parts of town. The majority of these people lived in the shanty towns where the bulk of the Central and South American populations subsisted. Wonder why they would do anything to get into the USA. Anything to make a few American dollars. some of them dying in the attempt. One moment at this dump would remove any questions anyone ever had.

I saw him on a mound a couple hundred feet from the track and I use the term loosely. He looked at the Rover like it might be a  dragon. No fear, only anticipation, perhaps in his heart he was making the dream to one day drive that car. If one of a dozen diseases , AIDS or starvation did not destroy the dream before his little hands could grasp it.

At first the idea was so stupid I almost drove over the cart but then it hit me what did I have to lose. He might have been eight. The Boy was thin as a rail. His face was that of all the other local orphans punctuated by great brown eyes but the face was also marked with something else. Perhaps determination forged of desppear. He smiled and saved his life. I smiled back. The wind blew his blond hair back from his face. It had been the honey blond hair that had caught my eye in the first place. The gift of a sailor or a street American perhaps a passing salesman. I am not sure he would even know. I opened the window the miasma from the dump hit me with the force of an anvil. I gasped at first. then waved him over while trying to get my breath. He tensed perhaps knowing I was the new heffey. Perhaps I liked boys, perhaps I had work, perhaps I might want to hurt him. Yet in that second, the steel like demand for survival struck

him and  he began to move forward even as he
decided to chance all. It took him moments to
arrive.  Only tattered shorts  covered his emaciated
body surrounded with flies.

"Si Heffey."

" Are you an orphan. Do you have a mother and
father. " I asked some of them had extended
families I wanted him to have no one.

" No Heffey my mother was a punta' He says
this without shame or remorse. 'The AIDS took her.
I am by myself with my friends." He motioned
toward other children now moving toward the car.

" Get in!" I say  closing  the window the smell is
now trapped inside making me nauseous. The boy
runs around the truck and climbs onto the seat. It
will have to be washed. This is nuts but then so
what? I forget my original purpose to see a man
who made canvas and drive home by way of the
town. We say nothing to each other. He is enjoying
the ride scanning the surroundings like a king. This
must be the most impressive moment in his small
life. He looks at me with hope. Perhaps I have some
work for him.

"I am very strong.' he says in passing. The smell
on him is so bad I have a problem breathing but I
nod. We arrive at the house. He marvels at the
sidewalk, the strong wood and steel doors of my

castle. We enter to the horrified face of the Woman.

" No! I don't have sex with boys.' I calm her fears, 'Bath him and put some clothes from the sale on him. He eats with us tonight and goes to school to protect your little girl tomorrow. "

I do not see anyone for two hours the boy returns scrubbed within an inch of his scrawny life. He sits at table and uses a spoon and fork having been given rudimentary directions from the woman who watches him like a hawk. Tomas's blond head keeps turning to the woman to gain reinforcement.

"Eat a little at first, enough, chew the food well or you will be sick because your stomach is small now and must enlarge slowly." he is told. He enjoys the beef and bread, potatoes and squash. I like my food although we have local fair often.

" Afterward he disappears to help with the dishes no doubt. Then he is sent in to me. I am following Brazilian soccer provided by the satellite dish. The Moppet waits obediently for the cartoons sitting on the carpet beside my chair. He stands uncertainly until she reaches up and takes his hand he sits and watches quietly.

" My books call me and leave the kids watching the television. After a long read the boy is found where I left him. Sleeping on the floor. Outside the rain is once again pounding the jungle but he is fed and

has a place to sleep out of it. That is all he asks.
Tomas is happy with nothing just the base
necessities. I wake him and he is immediately
situated a little frightened.

"Come you must sleep, tomorrow you will take
care of the little girl that is your job and to learn." I
walk him down the hall. He goes reluctantly
perhaps afraid I will take advantage of him. I stop at
the small guest room. It has a single bed and is big
enough for him. I take him in and tell him to get
into bed. Then I turn and walk out stopping at the
door to see him get under the covers. He comes
over and hugs me his body shaking as he thanks me
and god all in the same breath. I push him away and
look down into his tear stained face.

"Sometimes there is great luck. Take hold of it.
Then when you have much give back to those who
do not. Your debt to me will be paid. Be good,
learn, do what you are told no one will send you
out." With this he went over to the bed and lay on it
and I went to my room.

Since then he has been an excellent companion
to the moppet and I have had my very liberal
conscience leave me alone.

However, here in the hotel lobby the situation was not acceptable. So far I've only seen six old boys from the Firm and of course Pat Mason who was the 'Tech'. My stomach had a falling feeling that Turner was going to send six or so old men against a major military target and without a leader or so it seemed.

Chapter Seven - 11:15 Am , The Hotel of Flowers,
San Juan, Puerto Rico.

## A Differing View

I suspect that Turner was as right, as he was
wrong. He started out by making enemies all round.
In his normal gritty, whiplash voice he hit on the
single negative most liable to damage each of the
participants. Poor information gathering from some,
bad or late communication from others. Taffy of
course got the fact that prison still could be an
option should he not go along. All of the men
bowed to the Spy Master. Outside of Pat and myself
but then it wasn't much of a fight.

" If you're not on the team Mason you won't be
able to sot down all the drink you'd want will you?"
Turner snarled. Pat looked at him in the way God
must look at a stupid sinner and said without a
flicker of a smile.

" I've been sober for two years now." So much
for internal information flow. Turner of course
didn't bat an eye

" Then you'll do a damned good job won't you?"
He came so close to Pat I thought he was going to
be intimate with him. Then away before Pat could
reply.

" Of course seeing you've found this mess you'll be the fearless leader of our little operation." he turned to me. The our was strictly grammatical there was no way the Spy Master was going near this disaster. I will never forget that self satisfied martinets triumphant glare. You had to say something.

" I am retired you know?" I say just to see the reaction. His upper lip immediately starts to twitch and he gets very cold.

"There are methods of handling that." He threatens but in doing this he meets my eyes and takes a different tact. "You'll go because you believe in England and the Queen. It's your duty, shirk it and be damned!." He says his tone lowered and with the assurance of a man who knows.

" I'll go because they are my friends." I said softly. Turner pivoted on his heel at that point realizing he could not simply demand of me as he had in the past. Perhaps it dawned on him he damaged something that Granny Staters his predecessor had instilled in those who served him and ultimately Britain. The Spy Master like many other men in a position of power missed the fact that saying " Sorry, your all I have and England is depending on you!" works better then " Do it or else." A man who believes himself essential will give more then one who goes forward because there is a gun at his back. Believing in something is more important to an intelligent man then the potential of discipline on any level. War was no longer popular because man kind understood its potential end and who really benefited from it. Germany will vote in a Chancellor who has no platform, a poor prior record and is not liked by the mass but will do one thing demanded by his people he will not to go to war. Millions of educated human beings are against this war. They are out in the streets speaking their fears and the reality of death for no reason but the financial gain of the oil companies and those who will rebuild the target nation after the army has blown it to pieces. Perhaps they are aware that the American President has had the world squared into areas of influence and delegated to individual senior military people. That these people now out rank the Ambassadors sent out by the United States in those areas and are treated like potentates in their operations grid , especially in the weaker countries of the world. The same strategy used by Rome to control the Empire and it's surroundings.

For a moment Turner absorbs this fact and then continues on his way back to London .

" Good! Then it's settled. I leave it to you. Report in a week." He almost runs out with his two body guards following at the double quick not to be left with the soon to be dead.

" Magic.' Said Taffy  watching me with one eye.' All by our bloody selves and without a plan, we had a chance, now with flaming McFurson in the lead we're all buggered." There was laughter all around but I knew they felt better that I was there and  hopefully my vanted luck would rub off on them.

" You realize of course that place is at the top of a mountain?" Said Fish just to get it started.

" Yes and no helicopter. " Chimed in Lorning his tired ferrity face for once lit with a little life 'What on my budget? Are you daft? Rovers will do for you Lot" He does a reasonablely good imitation of Turner and gets a second laugh.

" If we did get a helicopter we'd have to toss the Queen bloody Mary over one side so Fish could slide down the other." Taffy jabs at the fat man.

" Watch your mind little man." Fish points at the cockney with good nature high dungeon.' I can't go but Jerusalem will. He did some time with the Trinidad Military forces." I nod at Fish and smile at the thin body guard. Who smiles back under his ever present sun glasses. All of the this only makes me realize that the group will work together as a team. Perhaps just to show Turner they are equal to the job. I have the weapon now. I must use it.

"Pat I want to be ten miles from that place when it goes up, that is before and afterward. We aren't set up to rappel off a chopper or sneak up on a hundred and fifty or so well armed men. If Turner and the Spaniard are right we're up against Cuban officers. It would be nice to know who's paying them and that also means they have seasoned veterans not some farmer with a gun. Real soldiers who have been trained in the jungle and probably did a stint in Africa."

"They will have eyes in those villages on the way to the mountain you can bet on that." Fish being senior man becomes one of the planners.

"And what might I ask do you suggest." Pat smiles sarcastically at me. It is he who must work this miracle.

"We could loft over a small tactical nuclear device and escape in the confusion." I offered. Pat Mason has one of those faceless faces. The soft almost white eyebrows overhang tired terminally sad brown eyes. Perhaps the sadness is from what he has seen over the many years he had served the Firm. As a Tec it is his job to make up what is needed almost at will, for desperate missions or know where it can be found. Pat as I remember in the day, before he started to drink, was counted one of the top three Tec's at the Firm. Divorce then a complete loss of interest caused him to be down graded and then posted to the wilds of Central America where at least the booze was cheap. Granny saw something in the man and I had always trusted my bosses hunches.

" Ever thought that this temple complex might have some value as a historic sight, maybe people still come there to pray. That this place will probably be around when we're all dead." Says the short blond man with the indeterminate British accent.

" I hope that's not prophetic " I say almost half interested. ' I didn't pick the target the enemy did, so unfortunately. it goes." I didn't apologize or bandy words. 'However, ' I became more consolatory, 'You only have to blow up the part that has the controls and the disk displays the rest you can leave standing as you see fit.'

' The bottom line is this. We go in by Rover. Old Rovers not new, blue in color with white UN designations. Those decals should look old and scratched out in places. Everybody likes the UN so we have a fifty -fifty chance of not getting killed right off the bat."

" Lovely! ' chimes in Taffy. ' and every time we stop for a piss, we can sod about running after butterflies with nets. That will put them at ease. Pull the other one won't you."

" No! The UN thing works. We have a mixed bag Brits, a Canadian, one highly placed scholar from Trinidad and Pat still has his Irish passport so we meet the criteria. Also we get two good scouts. The Spanish will provide them and we've vetted them. I think they will help a lot. As to the reason we are there. Our little group is interested in finding an inexpensive and environmentally friendly way of disposing of killer bees."

" Cryme! You're straight soded if you think I'm chasing killer bees." Taffy grows.

" That small thermonuclear device would be just the thing to wipe those little buggers out." Offers the ever sarcastic Pat. I ignore him and the laughter.

" We're in the country for three days max. Not much chance of us seeing a killer bee. On the other hand it gives the good doctor a chance to visit the local hospitals and help anyone with the wounds but others as far as his little black bag goes."

" So everyone will love you maybe they put up a statue. On the other hand why you goin up the mountain?" Fish asks , it's a good question.

" If asked we're evaluating the  natural areas of survival for the bees. If it gets too cool, do the bees set up house. Of course that's if we're asked but I doubt that will happen."

" More than likely they'll just prag us and call it a day. We get to close to the temple of the god's and they'll prag us any road." Taffy said in his cockney accent. There was no humor this time.

" You're spot on Taff , so whatever we do it happens fast and from a distance." I counter.

" Lovely Grub, And a quick dash for the border with friends of the mountaineers every ten feet.. We may as well blow the bleeding place up and shoot ourselves in the bargain."

" Pat will take care of the electronic problem, I'll take care of the dash for the border." I said while Fish smiled and nodded.

## Chapter Eight -  9:20 Am ,McFurson's Castle The Gulf of Mexico

## A Drive In the Park

The waves slide in and cover the golden sand for a moment. Its leavings are a diamond crested wake as the sun touches the water with its beams. I sit against a palm tree, which has made the decision to be more on the beach than off and enjoy its shade.

The final preparations are being made to leave. I wear a light cotton shirt and shorts with good hiking boots, none of which look like military attire. Our tiger grass uniforms, colour coordinated to the jungle we will enter, are hidden in the two tired looking Rovers with the pealed but still visible UN decals . The four minions of Special Support Services a tight lipped, shifty eyed lot of skin heads work untiringly in the garage. Of course my mechanic has nothing to do and shoots me looks of dissatisfaction from the veranda of his small house a few hundred yards away. He has customers with broken down vehicles backed up and they in turn will go elsewhere or take the time out on him. There will be no financial loss from this situation I have assured him.

"A man who needs his auto is not a person for quiet conversation Heffy." Thomas says almost to himself.

I am tempted to tell him that he is not alone with his problems but hold off. The ocean and it's loss would be a great burden to me. I will miss it perhaps never see it again. Wrong thinking . This kind of negative evaluation is usually a result of having too much time on my hands. However, over the last three days, I haven't stopped, so this bit of relaxation leaving Pat to take care of things, is highly valued.

I wonder what price you put on the sight of a flight of pelicans squadroning out to sea or a porpoise jumping from the blue water for the sheer joy of it, not directed by a trainer, an antic that makes you smile regardless of your problems. What price do you place on the brightly coloured parrots that squawk behind me eating among other things Chiquita Banana's fruit. I expect an American delegation to arrive any minute to serve a writ on the birds. It is this kind of monster company power overload that causes Chiquita  to go to court to disallow the few remaining colonial nations in the Caribbean to ship their banana's directly to Europe. How much money could an octopus like that loose. Chiquita owns the American , Canadian and multiple other markets. But then Europe has a little and that threat can't be allowed. I am uncertain how it came out but I think in the end they won, which is expected but leaves large numbers of Islanders out of work.

Money, paper for which we sell our souls day by day in the West to purchase everything we want now a new television, CD, furniture, 'whatever', a lot more of it on credit. On a good day Alexandro a small thin fisherman is exultant having caught a Marlin and can now afford to pay for a new fishing net. We in the wealthy nations have so much. I fear the fall, for it will be from a great height and with much devastation.

I hear Pat coming. The Tec has a short quick step. In a moment a bottle of Guinness is placed in my hand, dripping with due and his lean body supporting a large glass of red juice is settled next to me.

" Time to go, I suspect." Pat informs me, although he remains planted watching the sea through his bifocal steal rimmed glasses. ' We just received those bee keeper suits. Look like a Mars landing clobber and all. Guaranteed to give the locals the willies.' I smile and he goes on.' How you holding up and all?' He asks directly . It seems it is a question voiced by others and in need of an answer.

" You mean, 'why would I leave all this to go out and die on this warm pleasant day?' I ask rhetorically.

"Yes! Something like that. Must be hard losing your wife and all. Sure you're not going out with us to join her in the great beyond?" Now there was a nasty question but I guess a reasonable one.

" Funny I never thought of taking my own life. My wife really enjoyed every minute she was here. I guess that makes her a special case. I don't remember her watching the news much, I think it depressed her, she liked comedies. I know she wouldn't want me to leave and miss all this." I took a deep breath.' No! I came along to make sure you guys had a chance.' Not going would have been easy. Turner wouldn't do anything about my retirement.' The old Spy Master would have made a lot of nasty noises but in the end it would have passed. 'The problem is Turner would have found someone else more gung-ho to lead you and that would have been terminal. This needs finesse. Not that I ever had any."

" You know, some  people might call this little fiddle terrorism." Said Pat in his reformed drunk role.

" No! Technically what we have here is an unwanted military establishment, which can potentially cause endless problems for the host country.  We, at their request, will take it out. That's not terrorism! That's the use of mercenaries to get the job done you can't do yourself." I say sagely.

" Really and this little wind up on the Euphrates, what's that then?' he questions.

" Something that has to get done I guess. You can't stop it so you live with it. As the Spanish say. 'What cannot be changed must be endured."

" What the hell are we doing there then?" He asks.

" Britain was the last colonial power there, maybe the Prime Minister thinks he can direct it but he's kidding himself. The Americans will call all the shots. They'll get the oil, which they expect to profit from big time and a colonial war which they don't expect." The Arabs fought Britain when we were there and they will fight the Americans now that they are there. The Yanks could go to hydrogen powered cars, that would bugger the Arabs.  Oil would become maybe three dollars a barrel and the President could take credit for cleaning up the environment. . Unfortunately the turn over to the hydrogen cars has to be slow or they will have

twenty million people out of work, that won't help.
So it's bring on the oil and bugger the wogs.

You see the President of the US isn't really a bad
guy, just misinformed. He figures go in there get rid
of the dictator save 1,500. people a month from
being slaughtered and all the democrats will come
out and make a new USA in the desert. The
problem is the Arabs who had democratic leanings
got out a long time ago and those who didn't were
part of that fifteen hundred people killed every
month . What the Yanks will have  are mullahs and
true believers. No, it aint, goin to work but then
maybe it will, who knows?"

" This one's going to be thin run you know? You
ready?" I ask. to change the subject

" I'll remove the sounding post.' Pat assured me
' I don't know what your going to do with the killer
bee Cubans once we kick the crap out of their
hive."

"That will be taken care of."

" What do you think of our lot?" Pat asked in that
direction.

" Well of course there is us." I smile.

" Too bloody right, two nakered old gaffers who
should be living in a condo in Florida." Pat and I are
about the same age.

" Taffy and Jerusalem will do the job but they've never been in the jungle. I know Taffy spent most of his time in Northern Ireland probably fighting for the IRA. Pope Is a doctor, not much support there and poor old Lorning isn't going to be much help but he'll do his bit. The guides are tough and smart they are the ace in the hole if we have one.

" How long have you been blowing things up." I asked maybe to assure myself.

" I joined up at nineteen and they said 'Patrick my lad you don't want to be some mud digging, trench face. You want to be in the wonderful world of explosives. There's money in it my son if you don't cop a packet. Thirty odd years Tuesday and I'm still here. What you do before you became Field Marshal?" Pat countered

" Oh! I did marketing for twenty-five years." I answered it didn't matter now.

" Any good at it?"

" My Career! You ever see a real ugly woman?" I asked

" On occasion"

"That's her." Pat laughed.

" You know no one will give a shit one way or the other no matter how this comes out." He said rising.

" A writer friend of mine once said " It isn't the Governor General's Prize or the Giller or the Pulitzer that matters a damn. It matters if one person comes into the store picks out your book from all the rest and pays for it with their own money. Then that person takes it home and spends the most valuable currency he or she has, 'time' to read your book and at the end says 'You know that wasn't half bad.' That's the real prize and the biggest and you never get to see it. We will know and that is all that counts."

The border is many treacherous miles away. The roads which are more like goat paths bring out the best of English language in Taffy, who comments colourfully on everything in sight. At the border crossing which is on the edge of a sizable town the soldiers at least look intelligent in their American made uniforms with the old tinpot helmets . They have gotten the word and we pass through without incident. Pat, I and the crew go for a beer while the good Doctor Pope does an Albert Schweitzer at the local hospital. Given the choice of death to being in a third world hospital, I think I'd take death. Pope is able to help a lot of people and  he wonders later if we might make another stop. I remind him that this stop might be our last, that wakes him up a bit but also saddens him. If I had seen what he had seen it would probably sadden me too.

The closer we get to the mountains the harder the driving gets. There are no road maps and we rely on overflight and satellite pictures to pick our way. At the base of the mountain we pick up our first sign of company. One of our silent but well muscled Indian guides  slips off the back of the second truck and makes it up on foot his old hunting rife over his shoulder.

As I suspected trouble comes at the height of a grade. The Rovers are putting everything into making the crest when six men in  various attire accost us with a selection of A.K.47s and M 16s. The second guide gets out of the truck to talk to them although I am pretty sure they will speak Spanish. A longish man with a mean looking scar hits him in the face with his rifle butt. This action is followed by general merriment from the banditos. One suspects the question is how many do we not see. The chief thug, a squat man with hard evil eyes set in a wrinkled pockmarked roadmap of a face, ambles over to my window.

"You are rich? Yes?" He says in accented Spanish thinking we are unarmed or have limited weapons. The UN decals tells him so, he is wrong and that is all I need.

" Not rich we are looking for killer bees to help get rid of that menace so that fewer children will die." He smirks at this.

" Why? So that they can be prostitutes or work like slaves all their lives. We are the revolution. After we are finished everyone will have everything and be greatly happy, perhaps you would like to help? No! " It wasn't a question and the violence was going to start soon. I had the Webley Scott in my hand. The squat Chieftain opened the door and stepped back.

"Get o.....!" He never finished. I shot him in the chest. The Scott sounded like a cannon but was washed away by the staccato fire of two Sterling sub-machineguns. I shot two more of the lounging bandito's as they moved too slowly with their own armament. In a minute it was over.

" Casualties!" I yelled into the quiet my ears trying to react to the rapid sound change.

" We're all here said Pat from his truck Sterling in hand scanning the hill above us for a sniper. Finally our number one guide Raymond came out of the bush from behind the convoy to help his partner Salizar up.

"There were two more but they are dead now." He said in broken Spanish.

" See to Salizar, lets bury these before we have vultures."

" We going to make camp?" Asks Pat.

" No! This changes everything.' I look at my watch. 'We drive until we get to your field then we attack before dusk. Any chance of surprise is lost now."

" If so, why bury them? It will take time to get down here and then they have to trail us." Offered Pat.

" Unfortunately our cover may not be blown and if so the vultures will give us away, its a two edged sword. We'll cover them that will split the difference. To hell with it take their guns and their boots. Let's go!"

Chapter nine - 4:31 Pm - The Mountain Below Imtuepostichec

Gossamer

Arrival at Pat's chosen sight was a battle in itself.
The Rovers needed every bit of strength, pure engine power including Taffy's driving skill to reach
the goal. When that wore thin, tow motors with
heavy metal wires had to be wrapped around trees
and rocks to drag the Rovers up unbalanced  grades
and rough terrain. Failing everything else, our own
limited physical resources, cursing and drenched
with sweat were placed behind the arthritic vehicles. Our added weight was the final investment to
achieve the objective.

Pat had selected a small flat rock base about 40
feet long and slightly less wide. The vans were now
buzzing with instrumentation, small televisions
flickered in the darkness of the enclosed truck
boxes.

I sat back letting my high blood pressure pill
take effect while Pat 's fine surgical fingers quickly
put together a fleet of six black drones. Each mini
plane was thin to almost arrow dimensions but left
room for a powerful engine, a small but high recep-
tion television camera, fitted in the nose and a space

packed with a yellow white plastic which represented  enough base explosive power to destroy a block of concentrated homes. The engine and propeller were in the middle of the plane and added to the stealth technology. From my shaded vantage point I grilled Pat a little about these tiny planes on which so much rested..

"Will they go five miles?" I demand.

" Mate, these little buggers will make it to Mexico if I set them in the right direction, but to control them you need a five mile radius. See they run on Hydrogen. Dead quiet , almost impossible to see and accurate as hell. Should get the job done. ' He finishes pleased with his creations.

" The first one maybe the rest of them will be visible." I query

No! They come in one at a time and if I do it right we should be in and out in maybe 10 minutes."

"Won't they pick up the radio signal and jamb them?"

" That's possible but unlikely , The little drogges fly too low for radar to pick up and they look a lot like a bird from the ground. Anyroad this is the best I got. We can always sneak up on them." He smiled

" Ok, ! You're the boss but I want one of them to take a look at the place we shot those bandito's today. I want to see what happened and who is following our track. I want to know how far away the opposition is." He nodded in agreement. I had the two guides out one doing a circle of the camp and the other on the highest ground so we didn't get surprised.

Pat finally tuned the radio links and took his flying bomb down to the field that Jerusalem has cut out of the tall grass with an electric lawn mower. The rest of the crew filled in holes and made the field as flat as possible, stomping down divots, removing stones and filling in the resulting chasms.

All was ready. Pat clicked the starter and the little plane hummed quietly. Then without a bit of effort raced down the field and rose into the sky to a height of maybe a thousand feet. Pat then pushed a button on the controls and turned to Taffy.

"You've got it. Nice and steady until I tell you to make circles. The computer will take it where I want it." The sleek little Englishman nodded mesmerized by his view of the landscape. In minutes the fleet was in the air. Each of the men had a plane control but me. I got to watch the show from inside on the big monitor. Pat took the sixth plane over our route. It seemed by taking our attackers boots and guns we had fooled the Cubans into thinking it might be other desperados but their scouts found the

tread marks which told another story. They were
coming closer then I had figured. The officers
looked competent in their light green uniforms.
Their commands were mainly Cuban with a few locals thrown in. They were all well armed and car-
ried an assortment of the latest weapons, including
a Russian version of the laws rocket and lots of grenade launchers. They moved quickly but carefully,
proving they knew the jungle and the mountain in-
timately. The only reason they had not found us up
to this point was because they did not know our
purpose. The other planes showed small concen-
trations of troops guarding the most accessible
means of reaching the target. So far we were an
enigma how long that would hold was tenuous at
best.

Dusk had started to creep in from the Gulf side
of the mountain giving it a foreboding and evil
look. When Pat told them to circle and took the lead
planes control.

The little Irishman had spent hours looking at
fly overs and satellite pictures of the entire area.
The listening post was open from dusk until dawn.
Unless something important was coming then it
opened specifically. In this case we could see the
heavy metal doors open on the two disk areas offering five different sounders of various sizes in

each grouping. They could talk to God with that outfit. I began to worry that they would pick up our planes but the diminutive size of the craft and concentration on other more important things seemed to involve the enemy; at the moment.

Pat coughed slightly and took the plane in just over the tree tops opening into the area cleared of bush before the temple. He now flew against the trees inside the cleared area around the temple unseen. Then in exultation.

" There he is." Cried Pat. I saw him too. A single man walked out of what looked like the ancient hood that might have covered the exit from a subway station. This specimen cloaked in a white lab coat fumbled with some cigarettes and began to puff away. Pat had picked him up twice from the photo's and discerned the control room from his position"

Our Tec didn't hesitate the plane made right for the entrance way. The lab man was only aware of it by the wind it created in its passing. We of course got to see the dark tunnel then light a picture print of a room full of computer and other electric equipment then darkness. The explosion created by the drone vaporized twenty odd people working with the equipment along with the control room itself. However, the blast was contained in the heavy rock of **the temple and** while the roof of the ancient bunker come corn crib, collapsed the surrounding structure remained untouched.

" Chock up one for Historic Sights." I quip . Pat smiles and takes over the second plane. This he brings over the centre of the trees it is immediately spotted coloured tracer zooms past until the drone seems to take a direct hit and explodes.

" That should make them burrow." Snarls Pat. It becomes clear the exploding plane has had its effect. On the ground bodies are sprawled about the defenses. as the third plane slips into the area from the far left and makes for the open display. It is only sighted at the last moment and slides into the disk like sound catchers with an explosion which is audible from our present position.. The second display is now closing. Pat's right hand attack is faced with what seems to be an impregnable a steel face. Pat makes right for the display as if it were open. The defending fire now concentrates on the plane but Pat dips to the ancient stone floor this causes the defenders to literally fire on each other. There is a pause in the barrage just long enough to allow our Tec to lift the little drone into the face of the display. The explosion is spectacular and leaves a substantial hole in the defenses. The fifth plane now dives directly for the hole. Technology is awesome when used with this kind of expertise. The defend

-ers have no chance at all. The final plane threads the needle and explodes inside the display causing the building to which they are attached  to collapse with a rumble. It's over! I look at my Epsylon eight minutes 10 seconds.

## Chapter Ten - 4:50 Pm - The Mountain Below Imtuepostichec

### Run Like Hell!

I stand slowly and call them all to me.

" Pat destroy the vans." Pat moves to carry out my orders.

" Everyone else small packs, as much ammo as you can carry and Jerusalem you have the 710. The Schweizerische fired 900, 7.62 NATO Rounds per minute was built by the Swiss who knew how to manufacture versatile very effective guns. Jerusalem hefted a fully operational machinegun that weighted only 21 pounds.

I indicated Salazar should lead out .

"Wait a bloody minute! ' Pat charges back. 'We're going to walk through that?" he thumbs tall jungle like forest set on ridges and valleys that create problems, all the way to Mexico. I smile.

"That's right we walk." I wasn't taking any crap but then a little sugar draws more flies then vinegar as my old Grandma used to say. ' I have a helicopter." I offer as my proof.'

"So why isn't it here?" chimes in Taffy.

"Because I planned this fiddle for tomorrow morning early." So we're on our own until the dawns early light. You can stay here until the boys from Havana arrive or you can march and get picked up at first light." There is no more talk and only a little grumbling. The men now in battle dress heft packs and arms. I place the royal blue barret with the fouled anchor hat badge of a Canadian Naval Officer on my head and take my place in line.

In the jungle you cut your own trails, this provides lots of work but is much safer. The Australians in Viet Nam always cut their own trails and by the time they pulled out not one sizable Viet Cong force would go near them. Trail cutting bypasses booby traps, bungie holes and mines. It also requires the other fellow to follow you. In a different circumstance, I might have left some very nasty things in our wake. Pat was just the fellow to create them too.

However, we had three things working for us. One our night glasses were top form. Two, we knew exactly where we were going, the enemy didn't , which meant it would take them more time to catch on. The darkness would also cause the enemy difficulties as they would not be as well equipped. At least from our view of the following column from Pat's sixth and last drone showed they were sporting a lot of high tech gear. The difference was of course was how much they knew about the ground in front of us? What could we expect in the way of surprises?

The jungle closes around you like a moist hot blanket. Beneath it you strain for breath. Every action is weighted down and difficult. The sweat that drains off your body cannot be replaced fast enough leaving you craving water which when found is usually undrinkable. I have always hated the jungle. It offers  far too much potential for accidental or natural death. Predators are one thing, snakes are a second the enemy and their hidden ambushes come a close and lethal third. We are connected with short distance headsets that allow for immediate communication but these of course are for use only in desperation or battle situations both of which we hope to avoid. As a result, each of us is left with our own morbid thoughts and hair trigger fear. Fortunately the altitude causes cooling to some degree as the dark settles in. There are no swamps only tall trees that intensify the small movements around you. Every twitch the jungle makes, draws rapid response. The nerves tingle but that only lasts for a time. Constant tension slacks off to hard slogging over fallen branches, hidden holes and creeping  roots.

Pat leaves no explosive surprises behind. He does dig in sensitive motion detectors that plot our enemies movements.

It is the little surprises that truly screw up the situation. At a stream that must be forded. We find the enemy ahead of us, moving in small groups along its course maintaining contact by short wave radio. The beams of red targeting sights search for our motionless forms in the reeds. We wait forty five agonizing minutes until the spread between the small patrols becomes wide enough to pass safely but that in turn allows the followers to catch up. Time is now our enemy we cannot escape.

In war you always have a plan "B" if not you formulate one as you go along. Pat isn't the only one who has been studying the maps. The day before we left I placed a photo of a shallow valley before him and ran my finger along a line of trees that grew in a soft crescent across it's floor. He looked at me with those sad eyes and nodded but he didn't like it. The situation had changed and what we would only look at as a possibility now must occur and both of us would have to live with the consequences. In war you do what you have to do. I never expected this kind of dogged chase once the target was destroyed. There really was no reason for one. Obviously someone wanted to know who was responsible and preferably a pound or two of flesh to offer in exchange for they're own bumbling. Our equipment would tell them little. The drones were

only particles. They needed a live prisoner
something we would not, could not provide them
with. As a result Taffy, the two guides Jerusalem,
Lorning and I were dug in on the edge of the valley
while Pat made magic with the trees which required
the Doctors help.

The hand monitor for our nearest motion
detector blinked franticly as Pat returned.

" Right you know what to do. Do It" Not great
orders on the line of a Patton or an Alexander but
everyone moved to the predetermined locatiôns
required. Salizar, Taffy and myself were delegated
to kill the point element. Based on constant
monitoring that element had not increased from
four men all day. These scouts were placed twenty
to forty meter's ahead of the main body. One man,
then three more, then the great snake of followers
numbering fifty or more. We moved passed the last
trees by the proscribed distance. I indicated Salizar
take the first man. Taffy took one side of the trail,
further down, I the other Shooting each other was
not part of the plan.

The tree was thin but I crouched at its base and
removed my knife from it's sheath with a soft
whisper of metal on leather. We had camouflaged
our faces in black and olive green as warriors of an
older time might. I began to breath in small single

breaths. Air ingested through the nose out through
my mouth puckered to a whistle but
in silence. This is more for the relief of pain but the
action always seems to completely relax me. I wait.
death is to come to another human being by my
hands. One more, there had been the three banditos
earlier in the day but the Sterlings had part of that. I
killed then to survive. Perhaps they only wanted to
rob us but I knew in my own mind it would have
been our bodies found or buried barefoot. The rules
of survival are clear. Kill or be killed. I believe
though that man is more than a worm. A worm with
hands yes and who stands up right true but who
absorbs food and defecates, worms do the same
without any thought. Lions have evolved their claws
and teeth, spiders a web, man a brain. We live now
as we lived centuries ago. In caves of our own
manufacture true but caves still. Lit by electricity
but then it was fire. We can have all we want
without killing but others want what we have and so
we must stop them. Man to escape this morass, is
ready for a quantum leap. Perhaps a machine that
reorganizes atoms into any shape or thing we want,
so that all of us can have whatever we want.  At that
point money would have no value and man kind can
face the future which is in the stars, questing
outward until we come to the end and know the

truth. Now we are only worms who have learned a
few tricks. 'You cannot keep a black man in the
gutter.' Harry S. Truman said " Because you have to
have a white man in the same gutter holding him
there." Man must stand equal, jealous of nothing, to
look outward, until then, we will remain worms!

I hear the point man pass and remain close to the
ground, stop breathing pray. He moves hesitantly
stopping as if to sniff the air before going forward.
Does he smell me? But no he is off and away.
around the bend. The three followers come in line.
With one motion I open my eyes and swing the
knife up under the rib cage of the third and last
man. At the same time jamming the rifle into his
face, grasping his trigger guard to stop him from
firing. I am face to face with him. His eyes question
inches away as if to say 'is it true'? I lift him off the
ground with my next thrust fear giving me
adrenaline and strength. I smell his breath as it
empties from his now dead lungs bad teeth, meat,
spices at the end a moment then a sweet smell hard
to hold or even believe in, yet there and gone. Was
that his soul? No!

I am aware of Taffy's silenced Walther sounding
twice and the other two hitting the ground. Mine I
lay out. Dragging my knife out of him, cleaning it
on his shirt and I put it away with little ceremony.

We return to where Pat is hidden in a deep furrow behind a tree , Dropping into my preset location  giving him the signal and lie flat. The followers are just on the edge of our side of the tree line. Pat pushes the button on his control and the trees literally explode. The charges he has hidden in rings around the trunks are faced with marble sized ball bearings explode outward propelling thirty to sixty shot size bearings into the passing troops. The sickle like slaughter is instant and inescapable. The bearings going at fantastic speed cut men in half and go on to denude the trees on the other side of the path. There is silence then screams then a few AK's let loose blindly. At that point when the still living stand up to fire or look around, Pat hit the second button. The explosion is lower this time at ground level those not dead are now, then without thinking or mercy the third. The trees now are blown to pieces wood splinters three hundred times worse then shrapnel tears anything that is left apart. I give it a moment then open up with my Sterling Pat follows suit while, the 710 opens up to my right. We empty our weapons without any real reply then I hear the grenade go off. I know that Jerusalem will never return to Trinidad or Lorning to the Caymans. I turn and see the two enemy out runners looking in the machinegun pit and calmly cut them down. It is time to go. Taffy doesn't have to be told. Pat does not move and I go to him.

" Bloody stupid I caught one of my own.". he takes his hand away from the flack jacket and I realize one of the bearings has gone through it. There is no time, so I lift him with the help of the second Guide and haul him along between us. It is apparent by the time we reach  Taffy and the Dr. Pat can not walk.
It's decision time.

" Shoot him." Taffy says without thinking.

I place the wounded Tec on the stretcher and tell everyone to take a handle. We run.

## Chapter Eleven - 8:45 Am , A Small Areo Rio Hanger

## Redemption

I sit face in hands pondering the horror of war.  If I had not known it before, I do now.

We run four miles. Actually we stumble and curse while crashing through the undergrowth like a bulldozer gone mad. It is by Gods grace and Raymond's capable direction that we get to the small hill. Fortified at it's flat top by craggy outcrops  protected from prying eyes. Scrawny trees add extra protection. How we got Pat's dead weight up that incline I cannot remember.  I still have light pains across my chest from the last few horrible meters. After placing a small pup tent over Pat, I situate the remainder of my command in the best possible location to stop an upward assault. Although I figure none will materialize. At this point the enemy has no officers standing and what is left of their troops are in no condition to sustain a concentrated attack. Under any circumstances a frontal on this hill would  produce a slaughter and the followers didn't have any mortars with them so we were relatively safe for the moment.

I do my best to keep a clear watch but to my never ending shame I am overwhelmed by my high blood pressure and twenty-four hours without rest. I fall asleep and must be gently woken by Raymond who smiles and offers some berries he has found to break my fast..

Pat is holding his own but has lost blood. At the landing field just across the border there is blood siphoned from each of us and held for use. Here all Dr. Pope can do is change bandages and project where the ball baring is at this moment inside the Tec's chest cavity. It will have to come out but somewhere clean and safe.

There is a whirling to the north and I know that old silent Phil has come to my rescue one more time. However, it is a near run thing as the ancient Sikorsky Helicopter certa 1951. Just rises above the height of the landing field and plumps its self down with a wheeze. Its engine chugs ready to die. I run over to thank Phil.

"Get the hell in!" His angry face screams down at me. We scramble pell mell into the copters tired interior and by God it leaves the ground by some mysterious force having nothing to do with it's antiquated machinery.

The engine chugs along like a coffee grinder then coughs tuburculanly just to really scare the hell

out of us. We are also being followed. A white
Piper Cub shoots by sizing up the situation. With
the doors closed he can't see much but then he
doesn't have to. On our side we see lots of guns
inside the little plane and what look like
machineguns strapped under the wings.
A Cessna turns up a little later. Sterling's are placed
in gear mechanically but it won't be much of a
fight. The old girl carrying us will probably fall to
pieces the first burst we get off.

   Then as if on cue two Saber jets as old as our ride
but wearing the colours of the host country show
up. They still look sleek and dangerous with the
five fifty caliber mounts sheathed in either side of
there noses. Interestingly enough the Piper and
Cessna disappear immediately and allow us to cross
the border a few moments later and land
miraculously thanks to Phil's years of training.

   From my wooden throne I watch as Phil and our
four Special Services people work on the ancient
helicopter. They had better! It is to take them out to
a ship in the Gulf which will eventually drop them
off at Bermuda and of course Phil in flying range of
the British Virgin Islands. Camouflaged in battle
dress they will take our place on the helicopter
while the attack team leave in a Lobo's Meat truck.
I will follow in a blue Rover which is identical to

one of the two destroyed on the mountain.

For the moment while Pat is made ready in his hammock come sling for the rough ride to my place up the coast and Phil does magic to get his tired bird off the ground I have a few minutes to sit and think.

If I did not know it before I know now that war is completely redundant. I say this in that it has been stripped naked in the past day or so. If there was glory in it that has withered away many years ago. As to the right. How can you develop a good solid hate for men you see on television every night? Men like yourself. Women like your wife children like yours. In Iraq recently blue tickets were given out to the residents of Baghdad by the authorities. Each one was worth a months food. In one house though it meant life. A man and his wife sat with their nine other children watching the youngest girl in terrible pain over an infected appendix. Remember this is a country where you pay first for medical assistance. The man had little so he sold one of his cards to the black market. The money was then given to a doctor who removed the appendix before it burst. The child though thin made a reasonable recovery to the obvious joy of her parents. In payment for this joy the entire family all twelve people ate bread and tea for a month.

A man like you or I. Which of us would not sacrifice in a similar way for our child in the same distress. How can you hate a man like that? He is you. His leaders deserve retribution but I question if they will receive it.

War is and always has been a rich mans game. They of course never really participate with the exception of pulling strings. This said, who will die for the price of oil, the cost of diamonds the production of cigarettes ,tires or their ilk? Perhaps children or the uneducated for a hand full of food or low end loot.

War at least,  land war is a thing of the past. We had proved the terrible potential of technology. Our own small battle controlled so effectively had destroyed a much larger force with little difficulty. It is common knowledge that no land army can stand up to the Americans in the field. As a matter of fact it would be suicide for most technically advanced nations to do so. The counter balance to all this technology is that once you have control of the territory you want, the number of small arms and other weapons available to the conquered is endless. These weapons are not high tech but effective and easy to use. They slowly bleed a conquering force. Death by a thousand cuts, until it is too expensive or too costly in  death of troops and

the loss of support for the war at home to continue.
The old colonial nations found this to their
detriment. The Americans who have gotten away
with a lot of things in South America are trying to
take their show on the road. It will be interesting to
see what the results are.

I knew in my soul that I would never be
involved in this sort of thing again. Firstly, because
I was good at it. Secondly, because of the appalling
loss of life. I had survived Cancer how could I
extinguish the lives of others so carelessly. Thirdly,
and perhaps most importantly, it was so counter
productive. We have slipped back into the middle
ages fighting for land, water, resources which will
be more valuable as the population rises and the
amounts become smaller. Is it not possible that the
frozen sea of water under the moons surface might
be mined? What potential is there out beyond the
stars? We are cursed by leaders who see only the
wheat which will be bread, not the glory of the
actual growing of the food. They play with toys in
the dirt while we completely bypass what is our
future. Space and if not that at least peace should be
ours.

I cannot and will not degrade the investment in
courage and national loyalty shown by men over the
ages who have died for God, King and country but
times as men change. Did we not fight those good

fights to achieve a better tomorrow? Is all that suffering, all that loss, to be ignored? We can stop it. We can say we will not go. Perhaps then it will stop. Perhaps when we know the man in the next nation as we know our next door neighbor it will stop. Certainly a tired old courier hopes and prays so. The deaths I have caused weigh heavily on me but they cannot be unmade. I will make peace with myself I hope.

Taffy wanders about in nervous imbalance. He shoots questioning looks at me. Finally I motion him to come over.

" Look am I done here? " He asks in a surly voice his nerves getting the better of him. With what he's seen so are mine.

" Sure you're clear." I say without reservation. Taffey relaxes visibly

" Good! Listen I can catch a ride with a transport pilot." He thumbs a DC3 out on the field getting ready to leave.' He'll take me to the capital."

" Ok! Take care of yourself." I rise to shake hands with the tough little Englishman.

" Magic" Is his only reply and he is gone.

As Taffey walks out the great doors Raymond waits on the fringe for my attention.

I walk over to him and smile.

"You wish to fly away too?" I indicate Taffey.'

" No Heffey. I do not like the mettle birds so
much." He takes a side long glance at Phil's
monstrosity and I laugh a little.

" Here's your money." I hand him folded bills in
an envelope then a second. Salizar will not be going
home. We passed his body intertwined in a
gruesome dance of death with the point man of the
following force having stabbed each other in their
last moments.' See Salizar's family gets this." He
nods and disappears into the concrete for all I know.
He is gone. Pope waves to say he is ready.

Chapter Twelve - 2:45 Pm McFurson's Castle, the
Gulf Coast of Central America

Surprise, Surprise.

The meat truck backs in to my abode and the two
very competent men driving the van remove Patrick
as gently as possible. The door does not open as
usual and it is at that point I should realize there is a
problem. However, the situation requires action so I
unlock the door and direct the attendants to my
bedroom where Pat is placed on my hospital bed.
While Pope gets ready, I call over to the clinic and
ask for the doctors presence. This causes some
consternation as it seems people think I am dead. It
takes a few minutes to get the doctor on the phone
and at that point he informs me he will be there in
just a few moments. The difficulty with this part of
the world is that just a few moments might mean an
hour or perhaps never. My investment in his clinic
should have some weight.

I become concerned for my extended family. I
wander around calling their names until I find them
huddled in the boy's room. The woman and the little
girl hiding behind Tomas's frail body. The eight year
old is uncertain what to do he must protect the little
girl but not against me. In the end he stands his
ground.

"Are you well?" I ask.

"Yes!" We hid here they did not hurt us but we could not stop them." He says on the verge of tears perhaps thinking I will throw him out for doing nothing.

" The little one is well? " I ask.

"Yes! " He said confidently

"Good then you have nothing to fear. Tell me of this matter." I sit down on a nearby chair and the three of them sit across from me.

" They came yesterday and showed us a paper, Blanco's men, then they began to dig we could do nothing. Even Mariano would not come." He finished. Blanco was a local hood. He was ruthless but he knew I had relationships that should not be disturbed..

" Where did they dig? These men of Blanco?" I asked calmly.

" Out there." The little hand directed me to the pool.

I assured everyone all was well. I asked the woman to help the doctor as my friend had been hurt and he would need assistance. I told the children to watch the television but quietly.

After that I walked out on to my balcony to find my faded blue deck to which I had become so accustom with was torn to shreds. The outlines of four rectangular holes remained in what had been a smooth surface. The pool had survived though thank God.. The coffin shaped holes immediately brought the German's story to mind. I wondered if Blanco had found the treasure.

In the middle of the destruction sat the local Chief of Police. Well, the equivalent, as the local military was also related to the police and so forth. Pedro Feuenties held what would be equivalent to a Captains commission. He was trained in the States by the FBI and spoke good English. What Spanish blood he had, was limited. He was all native and so had moved up slowly on the pecking order which was often controlled by history and skin colour. At six foot an observer might suggest he was corpulent. However, he was also very strong. His hard native face was creating jowls although at the most, he was perhaps forty. His face was round not squarish with a large squat nose overshadowing a full mouth created by substantial lips. His hair was combed but just. He was dressed as always in a beige uniform shirt and pants. He had no marks of authority at all but you knew who was in charge from the get go. Like everyone else around here one paid a small amount into the captains retirement fund which in turn caused him to watch out for your affairs. However, Pedro was a decent man and didn't misuse the law too much. There was very little drug traffic down here so he handled the ordinary things that cropped up. The odd murder, usually some fisherman who found his wife had strayed and taken a machete to his rival. Not that the intelligent brown eyes that watched me with surprise didn't front for a competent police officer if required. It was just that Pedro didn't like complications and right now he had a huge one to deal with.

" Blanco had a paper signed by you to do this. ' Pedro said ' I asked politely." Pedro didn't want trouble with Blanco who had lots of pull locally. Not that he wouldn't face him if it was required but it would have to be over something more then property damage to someone who was considered dead. 'I heard you were dead."

" I'm not! Sorry to disappoint you.." I was tired and it was coming out.

" I didn't mean that and watch yourself. This can be repaired,' He indicates the rubble, 'relationships are important." His voice was even but there was anger in it.

" I'm tired ." I explain ' I didn't expect this and I didn't sign a paper."

" That is a matter for the courts." I laughed and he joined me. My chances of getting anything from the courts down here were next to nothing as Blanco had relatives in the justice system.

" So if you care nothing for my poor swimming pool why am I honoured with a visit?" I ask surveying the damage.

"You see the rectangular holes." He points needlessly

'Yes!" I answer coming to eye level as this is where the questions start.

" There were large black cases in the holes." He says.

" Did Blanco turn them in?" I ask off handedly.

" In a manor of speaking. Would you know what was in them?" Careful now the truth or ignorance which.

" I have no Idea." It's the truth and he knows it. Pedro grunts as if he was expecting something else.

" Bodies." He said it bluntly for maximum effect.

" Was there a grave yard here before they built the house?" I ask just to cover the ground because I think I know who the corpses might be but want to get around to the subject a different way.

" No graves! This is not consecrated ground." He snorts

" I've been here only four months and no one has touched the deck in that time. How old are these bodies of yours?" I throw in just to take the onus off of me.

"Old!' Pedro nods to himself.' No one is accusing you of this." Of course he'd like to, that would finish the problem but he too knows my connections and doesn't want trouble. To that point , however he sends his next test shot.

" I have heard that over fifty men were killed in our next door neighbors mountains and a very old ruin was damaged." He looks at me as if I will give him the answer.

"Government troops or gorillas there are so many now I can't keep count?" I ask just to keep it going.

" Mercenaries, they say, terrorists maybe? But one side went south and the other disappeared. They took a helicopter out to sea. The side that went south left a trail of bodies. Someone set a trap and they walked into it. Not just an ambush a real execution."

"Well if both have left the problem solves its self." I smile.

" If both have left?" Pedro's voice is hard and inflexible. If he is tied into CIA which a lot of them are then he might know, or then likely he might guess but I have done nothing, I am also alive which means I still command those links beyond the boundaries of his small control so it is finished. Pedro rises to leave.

" What will you do with this then?" He means will there be problems with Blanco.

" I will agree to the amount on the paper if it is not ridiculous and have my deck repaired. I will request that Blanco contact me before doing any more digging. It is a reasonable request. I do not see a problem." Blanco knows I have connections he will accept the compromise and leave me alone." He too knows of the fifty dead men. This number would disturb even him.

" He was looking for the Chinaman's treasure you know.' Said Pedro still probing 'The bodies in the boxes are Chinese." Padro says with certainty.

" They are Cambodian I think, if what I was told is true but the blood is mixed over there so they might be Chinese.' I said. 'When the Spanish were adding on the second level for Torro there was an explosion. Blanco rebuilt the place outside of the final designs which Madrid sent people in to do. He knows there is nothing in the house." I finish.

" Maybe elsewhere no!" Pedro probes.

" No! If this treasure exists I do not believe it is here. The rocks have ears here, everyone knows. No! The treasure is in a bank somewhere. That way you can get some of it if you want it. The reason no one has dug up the pool is because no one wanted anyone to know those bodies were there. You and I know the water table around here makes the ground spit up things from time to time. The concrete is there to hide the crime not to hide treasure. Those fellows you have, perhaps they were the Chinaman's protectors but once the treasure was hidden he could not trust them. " I left it at that.

" It makes sense. How is your friend. " Pedro knows all.

" He injured himself while hunting the doctor says he will be alright." I smile, Pedro grins.

" Did anyone else happen by to see the mess?" I ask just to see the reaction.

" Only the Dr. Sanchez to see if he could help but he could not so he left" Said Pedro knowingly.

## Chapter Thirteen - 12:35 Pm , McFurson's Castle, The Gulf Coast of Central America.

### Spying 101

The two doctors sit quietly in the front room and relax discussing Pat who has had his ball bearing removed from behind one of his ribs.  The projectile on it's way through has damaged some of his insides but a little meatball surgery allows the Tec to stay with us. At the moment he is sleeping and under sedation. The woman assisted but the local doctor brought the best nurse in the area with him, the bill of course will be astronomic by local standards, The  Firm's insurance will cover the whole thing under petty cash..

   After making sure Pat was going to be alright. I have a long but amiable discussion with Blanco who agrees to fix the deck  but the price which is obscene is negotiated. We both come out better so that any personal problems will sleep, I hope.

   Having done all I can its off to my bed. I have trouble stripping off my clothing the fatigue makes shedding my outer skin difficult.  First a shower, a long, hot, cleansing, soothing shower letting the jet spray massage away my pains. Having dried myself I go naked directly to the bed and flop face down allowing my muscles to relax.

The little things in the chamber remind me that I am home. I wish my wife were there. Being brought to the level of things which carry memories is a poor one but then I remind myself that Tomas is there. The woman and the Moppet are my friends. They share my time as I need them. However, while they may all have some feelings for me, they are attached to me by fear, not love and that is a poor way to be under any circumstances.

I sense the woman enter the room her delicate little feet make almost no noise on the red tile floor. The room is bright the curtains drawn back, its Spartan white walls give the impression of greater size than it has. The curtains are open but no one will look in the large wood paneled window, a strategically placed wall outside assures that. I spy her in the mirror mounted on the bureau. She hesitates at the door looking at my tired scarred body. Enjoy kid I'm too tired to care, my mind tells her. The room is silent The Woman stands there in her clean but plain white dress which just allows a vague understanding that she is naked beneath it's fresh surface. For a moment she thinks about the matter then makes a decision. I smile as I watch her small round face harden into the right thing to do mode. This look is one of her little traits once I see

that little mask form and then disappear I know it's
full speed ahead on whatever she wants to do. For a
moment her small hands are busy behind her back.
The dress is old fashioned and has a bow behind it.
With this hindrance undone, her hand snakes up to
undo the buttons and she gently steps out of the
garment. Her elegant body moves over to the chair
where the dress is carefully folded and left just so.
If you have little then it must be taken care of. The
movements allow her fine firm breasts to sway
softly as the her full bottom moves to a rhythm
which is part of her soul. She now moves toward
the bed. I might have gotten up at this point but I
was wondering what she had in mind. I feel her
weight on the bed as it drops ever so slightly. In one
motion she straddles my body and places her tight
little bum on mine. The touch of her flesh excites
me. Then she stretches out her small callused hands
to the top of my neck and begins to message the
knotted muscles there. This allows hardened nipples
to touch my back and softly make small slow
designs there, the whispering contact makes me
shiver like an electric shock has been put through
my body. Arousal forces me to shift slightly  to
make room for growth. The final straw is the slight
moisture I feel on my backside, proving once more
the mind is the most sexual part of the body. The

visions that cascade through my cerebellum are too much. I turn over while she tries to lift herself to allow me room or perhaps to get off until she finds out how her actions will be received. My hands pull her shoulders down gently until our mouths meet, her sweet smelling hair veils my face her breasts are now trapped between us we role as one person now locked together in lust. I quickly make provisions before the main event. Our coming together  was her plan from the start I suspect. The sexual reality is powerful and completely uncontrollable. There is no subtlety small body movements or special concepts added to make the mix better. The sex is pure and savage as the rain which now explodes on the house washing the gutters filling the holes in my deck, cloaking our driving , clutching  epox., which is a trembling, howling finish of release and total collapse.

I lie with her tired head on my shoulder drenched in sweat breathing deeply tumbling into the golden mist of post coital slumber. I evaluate her copper brown skin colour next to my bruised and battered white flesh and think of piano keys for some reason. She is sleeping a  joyful smiling moment on her face. She is fortified now in the fact that having been intimate with me and my satisfaction with that intertwining, her place here is better cemented. Perhaps it is just that she truly has feelings for me giving back to me what I have done for her in the one currency she has. Not for pay but with a little love. If so it is appreciated. However, I am not her man although I will protect her and her child there is too deep a void to cross to that point. However, after the battle this wonderful occurrence and its sweet ending saps the pain, fear and balances my tired mind. Given the occurrences of the last few days I hope it will be safe for her to stay. My hand reaches up lazily to touch her heavy dark hair. Messaging with one or two fingers I touch the top of her head and stop. For a moment I think it to be a mold but when I press a little harder it is not. Whatever hides there is rectangular and therefor man made. The item is just under her skin. As I press down experimentally I notice The Woman's facial expression changes to one of pain. My fingers skim the rest of her skull and find others.

"I want them out now." I say to Pope.

" Are you sure there may be wires under them into the skull itself. Perhaps I might damage her brain." The long faced doctor lists the reasons why he can't. He'd like a CAT scan first but we don't have one and the nearest would probably be Mexico City.

There is no time and its too far away.

" Now!' There is no compromise in my voice. 'You know what you're doing. I don't want the locals in on this for a number of reasons."

" You mean it's Firm business?" he asks some what surprised.

" What else? Also I like her and I don't want her to get sick. Those things are causing her pain. The kid has them too. Now!" Pope realizes the extent of the problem and makes ready.

An hour or so later I hold eight rectangular mini chips in my hand. Pope has made very small incisions and both mother and daughter are doing well. The small wires are removed and the tiny holes in the skull should not be a major problem.

I sit in my sanctum on the second floor and wait.

First, I have to place things in perspective. That isn't easy. You see regular common day spying really had little to do with our mission to destroy the listening station at the temple. That is covert or Black ops. Usually black ops are based on assassination.

More tactical action is normally left to the military. Turner had no-one else to send so we were it. That was the only reason I was involved. On the other hand people here in the village, a surprising number,

knew I was going on what was really a suicide
mission, in the old vernacular. The question was
how? The Firm might have a leek or Madrid but I
didn't think so. More realistically perhaps the local
government was at fault both here and next door.
Why did I think the whole thing was developed for
me. A set up to get me out of here to look for
treasure and to make sure there was little chance of
my return with the resulting questions. What did the
chips do? Could they hear sounds? Did they see
through the eyes of the person to whom they were
attached? Did they read the mind, give visions of
thoughts on a television screen some where? All of
the above? I had to know. I had sent pictures and a
report back to Ridley but received no reply. The
new digital camera really did a job. At this moment
the local Council General was on his way down
from the capital to take two or more of the things
back to London for evaluation. He wouldn't know
what he was carrying but he would have an escort.
Under the circumstances it was the best I could do.
Anyway it was urgent and he was getting paid too.
Taking them myself was out of the question. I had
a terrible feeling the things were wired and
movement of more then ten feet from the house
would cause an accident to occur to me. Maybe a
nice outright robbery with murder thrown in for

good measure, would do just as well. I knew there
would not be a lot of questions asked locally,
although as soon as the Middle East mess sorted it's
self out, home office would look into it hard.
London had digital enlargements to work with large
enough to identify every cavity in the chips which
should do for the moment. In the short run I had the
chips someone would want them back badly and
how each of us played the game would tell the
story.

The real basis of spying is the accumulation of
information. What I held in my hand was the
ultimate edge of that quest. To see into the mind of
your adversary or to clearly understand those who
might harm a country would be the ultimate
defense. The difficulty is where does that stop. A
well known and very out spoken comedian in the
States once said the mind was the last place man
kind could know his opinions and thoughts were
safe. Where he or she could think and have
thoughts about anything without fear of reprimand
or retribution. The eight little chips with their wires
sounded a death knell to that freedom. Think of a
nation implanted at birth. Every thought of a
population evaluated and considered. The ability to
pick out child molesters before the fact. Early
action on child hood mental diseases and others like

the symptoms of cancer that people will not talk
about or fear to trust others with. The ability to
know if a gene has gone wrong to replace it before
it becomes tuberculosis, Hodgesons or Aids. The
endless good.

Of course then it would also identify anti social
behavior and disagreement with the system. Then
what? Would that lead to the  conservative weeding
out of  potential problem makers. Action to insure
these people never rise above a certain level. The
removal of freedom of speech to insure the status
quo. What if the government is corrupt. What if the
laws changed so that anyone can be arrested
without reason and without recourse in law in order
to protect the state from terrorists in the wake of
9/11 are  turned over to a big brother equipped with
these little darlings. Those who crave power by any
means would know from your own thoughts who its
potential enemies are. I am tempted to destroy the
things rather then give them to the Firm which I
trust, in fear that some time in the future that trust
will not be warranted.

My one consolation is this. They can't work well
or someone would already be implanting the little
buggers. My house keeper come maid is only a poor
guinea pig for this experiment. These chips don't
always  work if I believe the German. The results to

present as they have to be charged with high doses of electricity to work in some way causes terrible mental disorder. How many poor people here who require medical attention have willingly  put themselves in the hands of  a Sanchez who fixes their problems and leaves this little thief behind to stalk like a cloaked vampire floating through the vistas of their minds.

One thing is certain, if a workable chip can be perfected the other half of the spy game will become redundant. Counter espionage is dependent on identifying the enemy mole or agent. A line agent must obtain information. He or she cannot place themselves in danger of detection so they have Joes. Individuals who work for them gathering the bits and pieces of valuable documentation. These pieces to the puzzle are then evaluated and cross matching gives a picture of the situation. The Joe of course is throwaway and will be abandoned if caught. In some cases where the line spy is deeply entrenched this can be very valuable. The job of the Counter Espionage people is to insure these individuals are spotted, trailed and taken out of the system. The scene set by these actions places two men in a room. One man  must crack the other and turn him over to double agent status. The English are experts at this form of reverse utilization and they have been very successful.

The chips would eliminate the need for this kind of thing. You could practically send a letter in the mail saying we know, we can find you, here is what we want you to send to the enemy in the way of misinformation or else.

The phone rings. I have waited for the call and am not disappointed it is the good Dr. Sanchez..

## Chapter Fourteen- 5:30 Pm,  McFurson's Castle, The Gulf Coast of Central America

### March Of The Peacocks

Five thirty is just on the outer edge of siesta but then air conditioning dispels a lot of the old traditions. The number of American companies coming to Central American for cheap labour, reasonable stability and lack of laws to hinder profit, is changing the major cities into small . duplicates of their North American cousins. Of course here in the village all the old ways survive in one way or another. Dr. Sanchez wishes to speak to me pronto. He does not say so but the timing is just inside the extremes of decorum or perhaps he believes being a North Americano I won't care.

My guest arrives in a taxi. That I find interesting because there are only two in the area both owned by a tough who is a minor thug. That of course is why there is only two taxi's and he owns both. The fact that this one is available to the doctor on call is not lost on me. On the other hand a flashy car can get you killed, we do have bandits you know.

The good doctor leaves the taxi and his body guard to wait in the shade of my car port. It is a nice gesture in a sense, it dictates trust, then again he

/

would never get in here with the body guard so its six of one and a half dozen of the other. I might be easy going but I'm far from stupid.

I am my own doorman today, Pope stays a few feet from the door. He is armed too. This might get heavy and the doorway may have to be held which is why Mariano armed with his greener is in the kitchen listening. For the uneducated a greener is a sawed off shot gun. The name comes from the truth that anyone who is green as grass can operate one effectively.

I open the door and stay on an angle to the taxi. The doctor smiles pleasantly. He has good nerves but that is in the breeding too. Many Spaniards, their prodigy in the new world and elsewhere have an elegant stance. A stiff bull fighter's bearing. I have always been impressed by this as it oozes power, masculinity and a certain noblesse. Unlike my tired self who simply oozes. Sanchez had that stance. It spoke of a man to deal with, a man to watch out for, certainly and perhaps if I did not know what I did, respect.

We went into the library cum den, which is right off the main door. I had considered leaving the door open but he will know the house has ears and so what will be said will be heard elsewhere. So that portal is closed. I figure he is armed. Most anyone who has more then five dollars American is.

I sit in a comfortable chair away from my desk, one that is easy to get out of. The location allows only my the upper half of my body to be seen from his position screened by the desk. He takes a seat which is softer to sit in but harder to extricate ones self from. This gives the impression that nothing untoward will happen . The Beretta in my pocket also insures that.

I offer a drink and a Cuban cigar both of which he refuses with the simple explanation that he enjoys good health and both might harm it. It also leaves his hands free and insures I don't slip him anything. I don't abide either and we get down to cases.

The man who sits before me dressed immaculately in a light gray, tropical weight, Brooks Brothers suit has less hair than he would like and tries to hide the fact. The few black strands left cover far too much space. His brow is large .and very flat. He has no eyebrows to speak of  but a large aggressive Roman nose which overshadows an equally large smiling mouth with very white teeth. His choppers are caps  but then he is from New York. His face comes to a point at the chin which given the shadow looks very much like it is shaved at least twice a day. The eyes are interesting, clear, candid. very intelligent. The windows of a crafty and intensely formidable soul.

" You have left much of the house as it was.' He seems to approve but also he now knows the lay out hasn't changed. That might be important for later. Fine lets get it done.

" It is a place I live in.' I close the subject. ' I am interested in why you wished to see me so soon." I finish like someone who has much to do and who is making time available out of courtesy. Lets see where that goes.

His face does not change perceptively but the eyes tell me he is disappointed that I am not courteous. It means I am aware, on guard and very North American. It is business first as always. However, being a New Yorker makes him ready for that. Although most people would be asking the good Doctor for free medical advise right now and I am not which is also an indicator.

" In fairness finding bodies under your house can be disconcerting.' He speaks with his hands as do I. 'I was wondering if perhaps it had impacted on you. It is possible you might need something for your nerves or perhaps some of your household are disturbed." So you want to be my psychiatrist and you think the woman has ratted you out. I'll just bet you'd like to see her for five minutes.

" It seems I have a strong constitution.' One down but you have to concede something,

'Although I was surprised. I had considered new concrete and Blanco made me an offer so." I waved my hands. Now that is a cold lie and one he would know if he was behind the game. There was a momentary hesitation. Perhaps he had expected me to complain about Blanco or something of the sort but he knew I was lying and so Sanchez was the problem. Treasure, money for his experiments what would a man give, take or do for it. I would figure just about anything to get a Nobel. I could see it in his face now. Just for a moment hatred, anger dissatisfaction , I had become another problem. I also knew something in my gut. Torro's heart attack was created not happen stance. Perhaps he had run his fingers through the girls hair and found what I had. He could have  mentioned it to the good doctor in passing. Exit Torro! A simple matter for a doctor with no scruples and Sanchez had none at all. The secret of his little chips must be hidden and he will go to any lengths to do that. He now changed pace to see where he might make amends.

" To be honest Mr. McFurson there are few people who could afford my abilities
here. I do work for the poor without recompense but I like to at least support my practice a little by being available to those who can afford me." Oh! Mercy me , the good doctor wants some help with the

terrible burden of sickness around here, which of course he is using for his own ends.

" To be equally honest I have a doctor. An old friend from the islands who comes in periodically and I have a good relationship with the local hospital. I believe I am alright, for the moment." I finish a little too sharply. His face becomes very intense like the matter he will pass on is very important.

" Cancer is nothing to play with. I have done surgery on many types and time is important as you know. My office medial facilities are leading edge. I have computer contact with major hospitals in the States. This might be important. Perhaps you will consider my offer." He finished like a good salesman.

" I would expect nothing more from a New York brain surgeon." I tossed this in to see how he'll jump. He is impressed I know as much as I do, but continues unruffled.

" I do very well in New York six months out of the year but I return to my own people for the remainder. The knowledge I have, I share with those who need it most. Am I to apologize for saving lives Mr. McFurson? " He was really hot but controlled it well. So I dropped the bomb and watched for collateral damage.

"What would you think of a man who placed this in the brain of a six year old." I tossed one of my little rectangular friends to the good doctor who caught it with one hand. Sanchez had good hand eye coordination. Did I expect less? I let the cat out of the bag because he knew his little attachments had been removed when they went off line. His objective was to find out what had happened. This would eventually lead to the Woman and her little girl so I took it on myself.

He studied the thing, his face showing the first bit of strain and some sweat.

" I think he might be trying to find a cure for many things." He said completely non pulsed.' A number of patients including your house keeper and her little girl were made part of a study in return for my help. I have signed disclaimer forms if you wish to see them." he sat back and waited.

" Interesting thing about these little fellows.' I play with a second chip between my fingers. 'They need energy to run. Lots of it. Which is fine if you have the subject in a room where you can feed it in directly. However, in  this case the little fellow has to work on its own. Its battery if you like  must be charged while in place. There is talk doctor, that

brain damage is the end result. Is that clearly
identified on your disclaimer? Sign up and I maim
you for life?" Now that was really nasty and
somewhere deep down Dr. Sanchez became
something else.

" Tests sometimes fail' He admitted arrogantly, '
however, I don't think the local government will
act. I am the Presidents personal Doctor. I don't
think he will listen to a shady ex-spy and
mercenary.

He knew about the attack. Sanchez had
masterminded the attack through El Presidente. He
needed the treasure and I was a hindrance. A bug to
be swatted but not here, somewhere else more
convenient.

"Oh! Wouldn't take this to the local government
but you might have to put off New York State for a
while." I smiled with a certain amount of my own
arrogance .

"You have nothing to harm me with and I have
excellent lawyers in New York, you don't frighten
me."

" We shady spies know people in low dark
places." I let that one float.

'You think I am harming people for glory don't
you? You are wrong Mr. McFurson. I am extending
the vistas of science. The trade you discuss allows

people who would die of some insignificant illness that we would take care of in ten minutes in America' He snapped his fingers for effect. ' to live. They cannot pay but they are willing to give of themselves to help the future. They do this willingly. You are looking for a mad scientist and you are wrong."

" I know many of the positives that result from this sort of thing.' I place the chip on the desk ' I also know the other side of the coin. Mass thought control, the breaching of the last line of defense of free thought, of an unsuspecting population by overlords who wish to create their own self centered paradise. That kind of power is a little too much especially when it is not being done in experiments in an environment  that can be controlled by a government who might actually have to respond to charges of inappropriate use. If someone is going to play god I'd rather it not be you." That wasn't a taunt it was the truth. He considered this for a moment.

" What you mean is not in the United States, or your country. A nice western Democracy where the game is played fairly, Yes?' He laughed then but it had no mirth in it. ' Your democracies have the power to cure AIDS with simple medication yet

millions in this country, the Caribbean and around
the world die daily because money is more
important than lives.

    ' In 2020 the number of Latinos in North
America will surpass the number of whites.
Probably much earlier because while the Americans
have great military power they cannot stop a few
desperate men  destroying major buildings in their
cities. More importantly they cannot stop the flow
of immigration into their country. The business
community wants the cheap labour. Very soon Mr.
McFurson we will control both continents. When
that happens I want a flow of the wealth from North
America's bloated society to these people who have
waited so long and still have nothing.

    " By then Dr. Sanchez with the present flow of
jobs out of North America, what you want will
happen on it's own."

    " You think so because you are white. Jobs
move because industry is no longer afraid of the red
menace. Whites will have to do with less because
profit not nations matter. Your society is destroying
the foundation that allows it to exist. You are
aborting yourselves to death. Your pleasures dictate
you not have children and you have the mechanics
to stop that. In the end you will become extinct.
You  still control the power

because you have the wealth. If we the majority are of a similar mind that can change. It can change through your own constitutions with the vote you created but do not use."

"So you're going to perfect this little gismo and put in the majority of Latinos and have them vote in a block for their own good. Don't you give them credit for reasonable thought?"

" They are uneducated but that can be repaired quickly and easily. Think of the knowledge that could be contained in one chip for instant use. Leaders, those with money, can be made to share. Politicians to make decisions for the majority not for their own pocket books. Of course these are fantasies.' He hesitated, then in a very business like way. ' I have taken up enough of your time as you don't need my services.'

Chapter Fifteen- 1:20 Am, McFurson's Castle, The Gulf Coast of Central America.

Offensive Action

I sit  in one of the padded leather chairs situated in the living room that adjoins  the front door. The house is quiet. The Woman and the two children are in her room at the back and perhaps the safest part of the house structurally. Mariano is in the kitchen with his shotgun probably raiding the ice box but that isn't the point. Dr. Pope is sleeping next to the sliding doors that lead to the gardens but his Sterling is at his side. Even Pat is armed although I am unsure how much he will be able to defend himself when the attack comes and I am certain it will.

Pat has also given me something to think about. In the midst of our preparation he calls me in. I make time because in fairness I have not spoken to him since  our return from the raid. I don't like hospitals rooms but also I have been too busy. There is a little discomfort about having sex while he clings to life but that is circumstance. The little Irishman is lying on this side facing the door and a small television I have had brought in to pass his time. The room smells of hospital. I know he is in some pain although the flow of pain killers through the tube attached to his arm seems to allow him to hold his own.

" Goofing off again Huh!" I kid.

" Yes ! would you mind sending in the nurse to look I have a serious enlargement between my goolics." I laugh.

" You think she can take care of that." I ask sarcastically.

" Definitely!" he makes the OK sign and then gets tired and old.

" You want me to leave?" I ask not wanting to over tax him.

" No mate what I have to say isn't pretty but important. I was the inside man on the job." He admits.

" Working for Sanchez? " I ask, " I knew it. The make camp thing gave you away a little bit. So you set us up and they let you go with money for booze."

" Yah! Too true. Sanchez is good he has these little pills that make you vomit every time you drink booze. So I am sober."

" If you stop taking them?"

" Then mate you die. I might be a sot but I didn't want to die." It was only for three or four days wasn't it I could do that. Sell you lot out and get my share of the treasure. I knew it was horse shit when the Bandito's, those were his people, showed up too slow and stupid by a long shot. I knew I wasn't walking out of there but that was the deal. I was supposed to get out and make friendly with them and let them cut you lot to pieces." He stopped and lay back waiting no doubt for me to kill him."

" You tied in with the people on the mountain."

" No! I was going to tell you not to camp. At that point my ass was in with yours and the others."

." What or who is Sanchez?" I probe.

" Now that one mate is a real puzzle. He's brilliant but cracked. This treasure thing was just one of a couple of things he had going to get enough money for his project."

" I know about the chips." I said.

" Chips? No mate, he wanted something that would balance the population in North America, I don't know what the stuff would do. It might be a poison but of course he didn't want to harm any Latinos
Maybe something like that sickle cell thing where only black people get sick. Maybe something like sterilization . He was negotiating with a lad with a real bag of tricks."

" Did you get a name."

" No! It won't matter much he'll kill us all now to

cover up. You helped me sport. You should have killed me on the mountain  but you got me out. Now we're a little more even. Too bad it was all for not."

Pat's information confirms we don't fit in  Dr. Sanchez's polluted future. He of course is crazy. Firstly on the level that he would think anyone would hide that much loot down here especially after the explosion and the destruction of the deck.

Secondly, this attack, if it occurs, is more to shut me up while getting those little chips. Sanchez knows the place is fortified and  knows I am ready to repel boarders.  He also knows that whatever London comes up with from the pictures it is only surmise. They need the real thing to make the final analyst. I also find out that our esteemed Council General will not be down for a day or so. The government has informed him that the bandits have been active in our area and his safety might be in jeopardy.  Sanchez has given himself some time to move and a cover for our deaths. I of course have contacted London through the Cleveland cut off and the Fishman will be in by boat tomorrow but until then I must hold out. Sanchez can't think we are sleeping in our beds and he has to know that we will be well armed. I wonder who he will have attack the castle. He's not the out front leader type more the planner.

I could have played it smarter though I think Sanchez got too much information from me. Belief in your own superiority and clearer intelligence overview will do you every time. It is however, a fault common to most people in my business. We think we know. The FBI thought they knew when one of their own was indicated as a mole. He wasn't but galloping paranoia and that sixth sense which is sometimes misplaced, took control. They tried to trap the non-mole with some stupid scenario which he promptly reported back to his immediate superior as he should and was required to do. This action instantly turned him into a master spy in the minds of the superior intelligence overview folks. There were a lot of red faces when a year later after the suspect had been really forked over. The mole turned out to be one of the people in charge of the forking. Such is spy work.

If I look at Sanchez for a moment and put everything I think but don't know aside. The man becomes less complicated. He deals with the poverty , filth and death every day we could not imagine. My house in reality is a fortress not of my mind or for my protection but to keep that poverty out. In South and Central America you can find tremendous wealth and human desolation almost side by side. People starve to death outside homes

where food is wasted or tossed out to be sold by
garbage men for pennies from the starving so they
themselves can survive. I am the Heffy in my
village because I have a few more dollars then the
inhabitants and I try because my liberal soul won't
let me do less, to help them. I saved Tomas to
placate that uncomfortable feeling more then for
higher reasons.

Sanchez who has been to the big apple and
knows that the poorest crack head can get a good
meal and help if he only asks while people who
work hard here get to die of some disease they
could survive but have no money to fight. So he
fanaticizes and then he works perhaps for years to
find this chip which will give instant education,
allowing him to dictate how governments and those
behind them will operate. He is probably in good
with any number of senior government officials and
presidents in the America's the New York Surgeon
designation and the university diplomas behind it
would carry great weight. Look how easily he set up
the mission to get rid of me. He has the mind of a
spy which requires the question is he or was he
trained as one. I didn't think so. My death by some
other means could have been created without too
much fuss. The whole mission impossible thing gets

it away from the village where the people who at
least have me, will defend that resource. Remember
he has to live in this area too. His chips are here.

If he can get his chip just right he could place it
in how many potential minds. How would anyone
know? One chip not four. He needs money for that.

He hates the whites because we are self
indulgent, slaughtering our own children and eating
ourselves to death while others starve. Something
also bothered me about the way he said 'much
sooner' when he referred to the Latino take over in
the US. He obviously had something in mind for
that as well.

It couldn't work could it. The right people
stimulated in the right way, fanatics who believe
because their own brain tells them. Individuals who
are not brain washed but brain controlled. Could
madness with the right brain behind it make it
possible? The Americans must know but then it
wasn't happening in America and while the
Americans, Canadians and others sent food to those
in need. In reality it was much more comfortable to
have the third world  where it was, starving,
illiterate and no threat.

I hear the car coming at great speed. The road led
to the heavy wood gates which allowed my vehicles
to get into the compound. These would stop a single

car but the main door wouldn't. I run back as far from the door as possible and point my Sterling at the entrance. The Taxi hits the door at sixty miles an hour but is slowed by the impact and the shattered wood that smashes the wind shield. I empty the submachine gun into the passenger compartment then jump to the right as dead hands guide the big brightly coloured taxi through the wall, my book shelves and furniture to come to rest steaming in the den. I hit the control in my hand and the lights all over the house go off. It takes a moment to get my night goggles on and started. In the back ground I hear the hard patter of running feet. I can see the two men who follow the taxi but they are temporarily blinded by the loss of light. The Sterling cuts them down. Automatic fire spatters in from outside. Some bright high beam light is focused on the door way I fall back . Mariano is at my arm.

"Bastido's!" he snarls through clamped lips. The shotgun explodes along with the light as the wide ranging double OO buck finds its target. There is commotion and cursing outside. I hear Sterling fire from the garden Pope seems to be holding his own. I pass the Sterling to Mariano. Who hunkers down to receive the next wave.

My body tells me of my increased age as I run up the stairs and move along the second floor. From the windows I can see where the attackers have placed ladders along the wall and jumped into the garden where Pope is making his stand. I arrive at the MG 710 -3 Swiss made machinegun with it's full box of ammunition . The window port opens

allowing me to set the gun in place and rake the bottom of the garden wall. The fire from there stops, one problem less. I also can see the entrance of the house from here and down the road. The second taxi is at the bottom of the drive. There are two men in front and Blanco talking to someone sitting inside the back seat. There seems to be a problem. I suspect it is the machinegun which was not expected. I bless the Special services people who sent it along just in case although we could only accommodate one on the mission. I take careful aim and empty the box into the cab the people outside are tossed about like rag dolls the man inside now dead falls forward against the door frame. It seems Sanchez's dreams will end with him.

I haven't got time for more. A new light pins me and fire tears at the concrete around me. I aim roughly where the light is  fire and miss. But then it seems to go out by its own accord. All is quiet. I wait it seems with the leaders dead, Tuffo the cab owner in my den the others around the destroyed cab the rest have lost interest. I go around but everyone is alright. Dr. Pope looks kind of white so I send him to sit and relax for a while which he does. Mariano still holds the door

" I broke your fine window. I am sorry. " he says and I look up to find a dead man hanging through the skylight.

" I can fix that how are you."

" Well it was a good fight and I think maybe we win ?No!"

" Maybe or they're getting ready for the second act." But there was no second act. With the exception of Pope who is grazed in the upper leg we come through with no casualties.

At dawn Artouro Moralies the leader of the Fishermen arrives at the door and politely asks for me.

" Good morning Artouro " I am about to warn him but that seems a little silly if he got up here there can't be much to fear outside.

" Heffy, I have come to tell you , that you have nothing to fear. The Fishermen remember your kindness. Your problem is gone. We the fishermen will take it out to sea it will not return. If you permit

Touch Not          (142)

I will remove those in the house as well so that
nothing remains but the damage and that we can
help fix." He finished and smiled.

Chapter Sixteen - 6:21 Am, The Beach Before McFurson's Castle.

Sunrise.

The sea was just becoming blue as the darkness began to dissipate on the horizon the light of a new day was dawning. The waves came sullenly to the clean white beach then slowly receded . I haven't slept for sometime and feel it. My body craves a soft bed but I wait on the shore as the large motor yacht comes in from  down the coast. Big Mouth Fish stands on the Port side rail and waves. The big man flew up the night before and found a trusted sailor to bring him to this beach at my request. Once he arrives I will give him the chips and he will carry them back to the next link and so on until they get to London. With the chips will go Sanchez's lap top saved from the wreck of the taxi plus all the notes and other data I can find in a quick raid on the Doctor's house. He provided the keys after all. On the boat will go Dr. Pope who while interested in curing himself feels it might be smarter if someone else looked at his wound. Anyway he has done all he can. I will send Pat along so he can get to a hospital. He has done his job; I am alive. Had it not been for Pat we would have all died. Perhaps that balances it out. I haven't said anything about his betrayal but it must be in my report. Then hopefully I will sleep.

To my right the fishermen leave as they have always left. The flotilla of little boats some loud some quiet move like a ballet across the almost flat Gulf. The sun coming up over the mountains which are the back bone of Central America seems to light their way out to sea. The boats are heavier today weighed down with bodies but that weight will soon be removed. Ditched over the side properly weighted down to insure they don't come back, as the tiny armada moves about looking for the fish that will sustain their families.

Earlier in the morning I finally got through to head office. Ridley is not in, neither gratefully, is Turner. The only person I can raise is the indomitable Peachy.

" Isn't Turner even there?" I ask, surprised that he would leave at that moment.

"Can't say I'm afraid National Secrets Act and all that." Admonishes Peachy.

"Well maybe that is for the better." I kid ' Bloody war or a sickly season Peachy you may end up Admiral of our little fleet yet."

"Good Lord no! I am only a humble part of the statuary I'm afraid.' Peachy plays along humbly but you know he likes the complement.

"Look, I finished up this Sanchez thing last night. There was some collateral damage to my house and I'd like to send you the bill as I was on company time." I ask.

"Oh by all means send in the paper work . I 'll give you no odds on when it gets paid though we're rather busy right now." He reminds me that the world is larger then me.

"Fine listen I won't take up your time needlessly. What I would like to do is pick your brain a little. Think that might be possible?"

"Certainly my dear boy fire away and I'll do my senile best to help." I laugh along with him.

"Our friend Doctor Sanchez what do we know about him?"

"Yes , I have it here waiting your call.' Paper ruffles as the old civil servant looks through a file. 'Right! Here we are. Sanchez was educated in the United States his family were in the salt business. Not rich mind you but stable. Had an uncle Endro moved to the US after World War Two. He was a chemist I believe, did very well. Single no children. Decided to educate his nephew, one would think. At any rate Sanchez lived with him  in New York.

Graduated from Columbia, Did his medicine at Harvard. Very intelligent, specialist in tropical medicine. Went on to become a brain surgeon. Very highly thought of. Seems you put an end to a man who has saved many thousands of lives." Peachy accused.

"Only because he tried to put an end to me." I say bluntly.

" Right ! You will write the report of course. Not much more lots of awards and so on." Peachy trailed off.

"Question there is a myth that travels around about a situation where someone put  together samples of the most lethal biological stuff the US had Anthrax, Bubonic Plague and a lot of things they don't have a cure for, new stuff. The story goes that some lab Tec stole the bag and walked out of Palo Alto or where ever with the thing. The Americans have been trying to get it back over the last ten years . Is that an urban legend or for real."

" You mean "The Bag Man" unfortunately he is very real. Actually he was involved with choosing the stuff that was to go. His name is Norman Godspell."

" How did he get it out of there the security is armored." I say amazed.

" Nothing,  Dear Boy is fool proof as we well know. Unfortunately some of the security in the US has its faults rather like Brinks before the big robbery. Lots of propaganda about security this and security that but when it came down to it. the place was a cracker box. Of course security has been heightened  dramatically but then the horse is literally out of the barn. Why do you ask?"

" How come we have all this stuff on Sanchez?" I sidestep the question for the moment.

" Your involvement caused some of it but he worked for our American friends."

" At Palo Alto?" I asked fearing the answer.

" No at a secondary location they were involved with tropical poisons."

" Would he have known Godspell?"

" Who?" asks Peachy very nervous now.

"Sanchez." I say a little miffed.

"Oh! I see yes they would have worked together I believe or at least been in the same labs  they interchanged on occasion. The Bag didn't come out of Palo Alto it came out of a third location in the area. What exactly do you have?" Peachy was becoming very uncomfortable. This was big time stuff and very dangerous.

" I'm not sure I'll get back to you." I shrug it off.' The report is on the way."

"Listen closely,' said Peachy in a tone I have never heard him use before one of command. Strangely your full attention was focused on his next word. Had you wished to shrug it off you couldn't. 'As you know I have never given an order in my tenure at this organization unless it was to place stamps on envelopes  but you heed this well. That Bag Mr. Godspell has is the most dangerous thing on earth. I don't just say that. There are little vials in that bag that could, if opened, kill half to three quarters of the population of the world not some single country. That is why the Americans haven't gone after it. They know where he is most of the time but have never tried to take him. There is some story that they pay him to enjoy the sun in some out of the way place and service his needs. Of course that only lasted so long. He has left on different occasions and played at god to some degree."

" You mean he spread that stuff?" I practically yelled over the line."

" Yes."

" And he's still alive."

" Yes! which means you are to leave him alone."

" You're saying this guy is unstable and no one wants to do anything." I ask flabbergasted.

" It is relative to the greater good old boy."

## Touch Not          (149)

Peachy pleads. 'Which is better, a few deaths or
millions? Now here is the order, if you have
anything on him send it in and leave it at that. If you
fall over him by some chance, Run! Under no
circumstances are you to take this man on !

Chapter Seventeen - 10:43 Am, Avenue of the
Americas, New York City ,New York.

Touch Not

New York is alive with energy of the millions
that live there. The last mayor, a truly great man,
made the place safe to walk and refaced or up
graded almost every part of the once rundown pile
The city with that rebirth has returned to being the
hub of the United States and the world for
transactions and decision making. Power oozes
from the pavement. Billions change hands each day,
phenomenal amounts of product is produced, even
the loss of its most important land mark cannot stop
this living power house from being the center of it
all. The direction of the day to day running of the
world is probably more effected by this town than
any other. It was on this tremendous personal surge
that I made my way to the twelve story building that
housed Dr. Sanchez's New York Office.
The office tower was old, built before the war
with real masonry. A farmer's wife  peered down
questioningly from the fresco over the door, while
her husband plowed the stone and crops
materialized from the future of his labor. In a
second panel they were culled and bound by the

strong hands of honest workers. It portrayed a gentler, stronger, more honest America or at least the vision of that time from the insurance company's view point who had paid for it's creation. I wondered if it ever really existed. Perhaps the farm woman had the right to ask the question, what was I doing here? My very presence might be disruptive to the very power rush that made me feel so right in what I was doing that day. The question did not have a specific answer. It was all gut and hunch. The old policeman's wild hair that does not allow you to leave it alone.

First it was the comment about the early Latino take over that bothered me but it could only be perception. Then there was Pat's admission and his inference to sterility. I wondered if Sanchez could pull that one off. A scare from some disease. Vaccinations all around. The wealthy white class injected more  because they have the money followed by a dramatic drop in fertility. It was all surreal. The problem was that the Chips were not. Secondly there was the single line in  Sanchez's itinerary book which read simply 'B.M at office 11:00 AM.and the date. He could just have a meeting with his bank manager or some other completely normal transaction of daily life. Perhaps it was a beautiful woman that he was to have sex with on his office desk .That might explain the fact that this meeting was to take place on a Sunday Morning. Perhaps a very rich and powerful patient with a problem that could not wait and who required anonymity. The problem was if it was Godspell he was meeting then  would there be someone else present who might carry through what ever plan had been laid out on Sanchez's behalf. I could have passed it on to the Americans and let them look into it. Ten years was too long for Godspell not to make a mistake allowing for his arrest. The CIA had too many resources. Godspell on the other hand might have placed one of the bottles or vials in an out of the way place with some sort of triggering devise that would start an ever widening avalanche of death and destruction if he was tampered with and could not check in on it.

In the end I thought of the 32 new diseases and plagues that had occurred over the last few years and wondered if Canadians had died at this mad mans hands. What happens if he snaps and goes off and does something really stupid. No! I had to find out if I was right. If not I had lost plane fare to the United States and back. If there was a meeting, then I would at least be able to make my pitch to the powers that be, to stop what could be the beginning of something really terrible.

There was security but a nod as I pass is all that is required, I made for the elevator. There was no response from the uniformed guard behind the desk. A few workers were coming and going. Weekend office time seemed to be a rule of survival in New York as in most cities. The security guard is more for information then a means of keeping people out. Dressed in a suit and tie covered with a new rain coat and carrying a leather briefcase I simply fit in as I had for fifteen years. The elevator was empty but for myself it was wood lined and smelled of wax.. The eleventh floor was mainly doctors offices, I checked before coming up. There was no one around. I walked down the hall checking each door until I found Sanchz's portal with his name engraved into the wood in gold. Nothing like permanence to secure the patience's trust.

The key that should fit did and I entered. There might have been a secretary but no. The large waiting room yawned open to greet me. A pile of aging magazines sat between two huge leather couches. Private leather chairs surrounded a second table but the area was not built for a large number of patients. To the right beside the secretary's desk was a lunch cum coffee room. In the far wood paneled wall was a second door this was his office and a second key gave entrance. The security was lax because there were no drugs in the office. I know this because it is posted outside.

The desk is large but immaculate as the man, no paper mars its surface but you know by the fine dust layer it has not been used. The cleaning crew, perhaps knowing he won't be here for months, does not do the same job it might if Sanchez were to show up tomorrow. This means he is unexpected.

The view from the large glass windows behind the desk is other office buildings not very impressive. But then the rent on this place for a month probably would pay for my castle out right. There are rich, heavy, burgundy drapes to allow privacy for the patients who are examined. I take the opportunity to close these darkening the room and my position behind the desk. The leather chair is very comfortable. A single light by the door will allow me to see who enters before their eyes become accustom to the gloom.

Time is a strange commodity those who have a great deal or think they have and waste it. Those of us who have had a major disease and dodged the bullet  have less and make the most of it. If only the Firm would stop dumping my old job on me. However, I am most alive when doing what I do. I am, I must admit, becoming adequate at this part of my life. That is when you get lazy and of course dead.

I am sitting here because hanging out in the hall is a dead give away, also I don't know who I am looking for. There seems to be no picture of Godspell and Peachy isn't going to help, so I have to determine who the guy is, confrontation is the only way.

While waiting I consider another discovery made for me by The Woman. She comes to me after my run in with Sanchez and Blanco carrying a small metal box. It has the texture of brass but seems much stronger. It had to be. During the rebuilding of the house by the Spanish for Torro, Blanco had created an explosion. This in turn had sent rubble over a wide area. The box was part of that debris. The Woman had come across it because at that time she was living with Mariano's family behind the old service station waiting for the house to be finished. Metal always has value and the box might have money in it. However, on opening it she found only keys. These she offered me as I was the real owner and they might have some value. The key I held in my hand came from one place only, the lockers at Central Station in Montreal, Quebec, Canada. I knew this because at one time I lived there in my youth. The red coloured plastic and the shape are unique. It seemed that Mr. Kei had left his treasure behind by mistake or design. I was weighing this information when the door opened in the outer office.

I sit stunned the Webley Scott smoking in my hand the smell of cordite in my nostrils. The body lays on it's face in an expanding pool of blood. One arm is outstretched fingers inches from the closed, still intact vile that has landed two inches from the hard wood on the heavy Persian carpet. The bag lies beside the corpse. Strange what the mind does in certain circumstances. I find that I am unimpressed with the bag, which is really a large metal affair that looks like an accountant's brief case. A case made large for wide files.

It strikes me I should be dead. As a matter of fact bodies should be dropping all over the place. My fevered mind flashes through the circumstances of the last few moments.
Godspell appears at the door and enters completely unafraid.

" Mr. Godspell?" I say in what I hope will pass for a Latin accent.

" Who the hell are you?" H e asks his square face hard and demanding but showing no fear. It is an every mans face framed by glasses, fattish, with a small mouth, small nose and large brown eyes.

" Are you Mr. Godspell?" I counter to gain time.

" Yes! who the hell are you?" He asks again uncertain now.

" Please put the bag down." I ask reasonably.

" See this!." The vile of yellow green liquid is in his stocky hand ' Fire at me, this breaks, half the city dies. Want to play?' he moves toward the door. 'I am leaving don't...." He never finishes the statement. My finger slips. It is purely responsive muscle twich, not demanded by my brain, just a fight or run response done automatically, regretted immediately but done anyway. I had decided to let him go.

The heavy forty -four slug hit him squarely in the nose killing him instantly. I had aimed at his face afraid he is armored. The impact slams him against the door frame which pitches him forward. I watch in horrified fascination as the vial falls through the air coming to rest on the carpet instead of exploding into flying glass shards.

Chapter Eighteen - 11:01 Am, Dr. Sanchez's office ,
New York, New York.

From A' to B

For a few moments I sat quit still, perhaps
waiting for death to gather me in. Undertakers talk
of the harvest when they speak of those who have
died and come to them for burial. When I didn't
become terminal my survival instincts dropped into
gear and I moved. First the vial. I took all the tissue
from the box on the desk and very carefully
wrapped the glass tube in the soft sheets, there was
no seepage. I then wrapped the bundle of tissues in
two thick blue towels from the coffee room and
placed the whole thing in my brief case.

No one had come so far but that didn't mean
someone hadn't heard the shot. I didn't bring a
silencer if you can imagine that. The last thing I
needed was the police. I have great respect for the
New York Police Department but no matter what I
said, after all they had a murder on their hands, they
would of course take the bag and open it. At that
point we were all doomed. The Bag had to get
somewhere safe. I took out my satellite link phone
placing the head set on and called the CIA closed

number through the Cleveland cut off. The cut off
gave me a secure line and direct linkage with Dell
Gray one of the few men I trust in this world.

It takes time to get through so I check the hall
way to find it is empty. Having locked the office
door I leave with a brief case in either hand while
this cut down my ability to defend myself. I could
not take a chance on dropping this lethal cargo.
Dells voice is very far away. the Middle East
perhaps but that had no interest for me at this point.

"Do you know what time it is?" He demands
having been waken from the ten minutes of sleep he
was allowed.

"How is the desert this time of year?" I ask. I
feel giddy a bad sign.

"This isn't funny." He snarled, I thought he
might hang up so I got straight to the point.

" You ever hear of a guy named Godspell?

" Yes… "he says sensing something terrible is
about to be dumped in his lap. So I dump away.

" Well he had an accident." I push the button on
the elevator and hear it come up.

" What kind of accident?" Dell's voice is so
tense it twangs.

" Terminal." The elevator opens and is empty I
walk in and push the button.

" Jesus Christ on a flat car!" Dell says almost involuntarily. He has a bag." He starts.

" I have the bag.' I tell him where I am. ' You better get your plumbers in here and tell them to go slow because I didn't check him for booby traps." I'm almost at the main floor and I'm leaving the building. I want you to direct me to the nearest CIA office to my location. I know you have something down town here."

" You're going to walk through New York City with that. Listen stop don't go out."

" I don't have a choice. The Police, if they arrive, and you don't get through to them, are going to open that bag. I won't let that happen. Secondly, I just killed someone and I don't need to play twenty questions. We both know it had to be done but that isn't going to change anything unless you have time to fix it."

"Who says I'm going to."

" Look I haven't got time for this. I am about to enter the streets of a city containing eight million people  carrying the equivalent of an atomic bomb, help me." It was a plea I was strung out too. 'You should have people watching Godspell just point them out to me. I'll ride in with them."

" We lost him," Dell reports after conciliation." He gets real cute in the subway system. Listen  the closest office we have and it's a substation is twenty blocks. Don't be a bone head take a cab."

"Dell if you were me would you take a cab? Random choice is one thing but given the cabby population in this town, I could be riding with Terrorist Inc. Which way do I turn I'm in the street."

" Hell no one lives for ever. Alright here we go turn right no left."

" Dell don't do this to me."

" Left." I start out. Perhaps I should have ·thought about the potential of what I was carrying. One! Just one of these vials with the right dosage might kill everyone on the planet. Now there is a cheery thought. The insanity of mankind being able to illuminate itself made my walk a lot less insane. I worried about everyone who came near but looked straight ahead walking as aggressively as possible never look like a victim. The worry that most haunted my mind was that a trip would change the direction of world history. No one bothered me. In the end I simply concentrated on placing one foot in front of the other trying to ignore the pains in my chest from the crushing tension and fear. Watching the traffic carefully. How could I be here ? How could I have chosen one of the world's most deadly sins to carry  like a cross to my own mountain of skulls. All this time Dell tried to help giving simple directions checking with me on what I saw where I was. He tried the odd bad joke. It helped.

I didn't see the van at first then the two SUVs that moved in pace with me. The well dressed young men with the wires coming out of their ears who walked many feet behind me, the two that lead the way. No one came near me.

In the end the squat CIA building came into view they had stopped traffic for me to walk across the street to the shear delight of the waiting motorists. Rest assured the comments were humorous in a sarcastic Big Apple way but I did not hear them . I was praying now just to make it to the door. The last few feet I wasn't sure I would. I felt like a marathoner who has hit the wall but mechanically with all the determination I could muster. I made it through the doors of the lobby and made for the elevator to the fifth floor. Two agents stood on either side of the empty box to insure my privacy and I was genteelly placed in the CIA's turf. I walked to the desk. Where a man in his fifties fidgeted in what looked like a pajama shirt and jeans. The shop director stood sweating, he had just arrived by helicopter. I asked him to  take the phone from my lapel and talk to Dell I could listen in to the conversation on my head set. speaker. Dell confirmed I was OK and I asked where The senior agent wanted the bag.

I was taken to the rear of the office complex to a large walk in safe. I took two steps inside and placed the bags on the floor and then as if frightened they might close the door behind me. I ran out and sat down in the first chair I came to.

Madex the senior man closed and locked the door in my presence. With my face in my hands I cried. I cried for the village of decent people where I should be. Had I not come what if that mad man had set one of his vials there? No! I had done what I could for the moment that was enough.

A great weight fell from me my chest expanded and the pain in my shoulders dissipated. I had saved the world. Well, I had removed one of the most deadly aspects of it.

I am given two chemical showers the first with my clothes on. The second naked. I am then placed in scrubs and a pint of blood is removed or at least it seems that way. I am checked out by two highly competent and highly agitated doctors who could have been home sleeping this morning. They of course are not told the why of their extradition from bed. I am also given a CAT scan. Three hours later I lie in a quiet room in scrubs waiting for the inevitable debriefing.

The fresh faced man who entered sat at the table so I followed suit. Once I told him the story he

looks for details. After  two different sessions I call
a halt to it and won't play anymore.

Senior agent Daily looks at me and is mad.
" You could have killed everyone in this city
today. My family lives here, hero."
" My family live in Canada and their having
some difficulties of their own right now did that
originate from Godspell's bag of tricks.' That
stopped him.' You can't tell me because you don't
know what is in that Pandora's box. Well let me tell
you something that bag has been out there for ten
years. I just saved lives all over the planet and I
would do it again in a minute." That brought our
conversation to an end. I am told that the final
decision went to the White house. The President
remembered my help with the cancer machines and
gives me a clean bill of passage. I can come back to
the United States any time I want, as long as I stay
retired. I am suited out in a good Brooks Brothers
off the rack and suitable accruements including
Bostonian shoes which are worth about four
hundred dollars a pair US. Suitably attired I am
driven to the airport and sent on my way back to
Central America. A red rocket meets me at the
plane courtesy of the CIA. Turner is very unhappy, I
have disobeyed orders but also brought great glory
to the shop so while he is willing to over look the

incident he will not pay for repairs to my home in
the Americas.

**Chapter Nineteen - 10:15 Am, The 20 Highway to Montreal.**

Home From The Wars.

We sweep past Dorval and Lachine crossing the West Island on Highway 20 through an octopus of connecting roadways finally crossing the city by the tunnel thereby missing the downtown towers and Old Montreal. Our destination is Montreal East where the majority of my relatives the D'Ivervilles live. Marcel my first cousin and a lieutenant with the Montreal police force had picked us up at the Airport and was taking me home.

It is Christmas Day. The windows are alight with the festive warmth that radiates out into the bitter cold of the snow covered day. We arrive at my aunt Lillie's home and are immediately taken into the front room, given a drink and made part of the afternoon. Gifts are exchanged, the children including Tomas and the Moppet open new toys and dolls. They are at first a little uncertain to be part of the fun but are soon dragged off to play with the other kids. My uncles and cousins pass through as they come off or go on duty. The majority of the family are part of the police force. While the news of the day is argued over in the front room by the men. The kitchen is full of the wonderful smells including three turkeys, huge pots of mashed potatoes and side dishes. There are thirty-four of us by supper time. We eat in shifts mainly in family groups. The family fills up on enormous amounts of mouth watering Christmas specialties.

The humour is rough but fun. The Woman speaks the little English she has learned from me but seems to be in cync with the Quebecque French which is loud, fast and joyful. After huge amounts of food including some of the finest pastry on earth the men wander through to the living room to sit and sleep off the effects of seasonal gluttony. I sit with my uncles and cousins seeing my mother in their faces and realize I truly love these people. Not because of my wife's passing but because they are part of and reenact my childhood. It was here I was always accepted and loved. Although, like all children, I crossed the line on occasions and was put in my place quickly it was always equally quickly forgotten.

It was at my uncle Leonard's house that I learned the true meaning of hospitality.
While Leonard was not well educated he worked hard in a plant and there was always good food at his table. It was at Christmas that he went all out to prove his real worth. Many is the time I heard him

wandering about asking everyone regardless of age.

"What can I get for you my dear?" Whatever was requested was immediately provided. I remember him speaking to my father who he called the 'Le Grand Ecoss'

"I tell you my dear, If you come to my house. You eat and you drink, you make me happy because you are happy." It is a lesson I hope I have not forgotten over the years from that good hearted man that I loved so much.

Everyone having eaten and the bulk of the food slept off out came the card tables and the sides were chosen for Rummy 500. Each year Uncle Leonard and my Uncle Gill got together as partners for this battle royal. I can still see my rotund uncle Gill going thirteen  no trump to out bid everyone and get the kitty which sat invitingly in the center of the table. It was at this point that Uncle Lenoard would drop his cards look at his partner as if he was insane, run his callused hand down his long face and shake his head. Of course Gill would get the kitty. Leonard would have the one trump he needed and they would scrape through to the chagrin of their opponents usually my father who really didn't take the game too seriously. All of these memories washed over me. For those men are now ghosts in my mind. The Catholic Church in Quebec is dying.

There aren't even enough people to support the few
priests left. The average Quebecois family unlike
the D'Iverville, are becoming small and
fragmented. The day I had just witnessed is passing
into the history of big families, strong religious
regiment and heavy moral control; although I
remember at one of my uncle's wedding driving in
one car while another came close enough to pass a
partially full bottle of booze to ours, this at seventy
miles an hour. No one said the family didn't have a
wild side.

It is time for me to take a walk with Marcel. He
puts down his glass and trades insults with one of
my uncles as he goes through the door. The cold
sharpened us up real fast.

"I'll make this fast." I say dragging on my
gloves. The wind is almost non-existent. The cold is
knife sharp in the nostrils and any exposed skin. It
is wonderful to drag great amounts of pure clean air
into the lungs. It reminds me of hockey games
played in the dusk of a late winter day frozen
through but coming home happy my cheeks red
with health and enjoyment. I have come a long way
from that little boy.

" Take your time it was hot in there. I can't drink
like I could you know?" He admits.

" Who can? ' I agree 'They followed us like I figured from the airport?.' I ask.

" Oui!"  We picked them up for spitting on the street. It will be very difficult for them to get out you can't get a lawyer today.  You're Cambodians, why do they want you?"

"It's a long story  but I have to find out if something they want is where I think it is. I hope so. Kie thinks the stuff he is looking for is hidden in my house. I want to stop them from trying something stupid like kidnapping. This guy has no sense of humour at all." Of course Sanchez was willing to spend twelve men's lives in a desperate attempt to obtain the  money to pay off our Mr. Godspell for what I don't even want to think about. How much more intense could my friend Mr. Kei Junior's interest be and what lengths he would go to? I had to clear this one up so I could go home in peace.

" I need about an hour without our friends tomorrow." I request.

" No problem . I hope those guys don't get bored looking at jail walls?" Marcel was a good man.

As we headed back to the house I went over my interview with the esteemed Mr. Kie Junior.

Three days after returning from New York I

received two guests, one I expected, one I didn't. Pedro Fuentis stopped by mad as hell.

" I want very much to get my hands on that Punta Sanchez." He spit out.

" I thought he was a great life saver." I say sarcastically.

" He not only put one of those things on my head but my little girl." Pedro is really angry. ' Also I wish to thank you on the part of our President." he says offhandedly

" I don't think you have to worry about Sanchez anymore."

" Strange that Touco , Blanco and Sanchez disappear on the night someone tries to break into your house." Pedro probes.

" Pedro, who would have asked if I had been killed or disappeared that night? Very few people." The captain agrees with me with a nod and departs without much more being said. I have made enemies as both Blanco and Touco have friends but the cost of potential  problems with me tend to be large enough to curtail retaliatory action. Sometimes it seems a bad reputation is of value to one who enjoys solitude.

I lie on the couch, find a soft place and start to read my book a second time. I am on the edge of sleep when The Woman comes in, the trip and the

situation in New York has taken a great deal out of
me. Every time I think about that walk my high
blood pressure rises. I placate myself in that
because I didn't look in the bag. It might have been
Godspell's lunch or his rock collection. I don't want
to know. Nor do I want to know why that demented
man was allowed to wander around for ten years.
It's done and I'm clean out of good deeds.

The woman asks if I will see a Mr. Kei. she uses
uses the local slang for Chinese.
I can tell by her movements she is really afraid.
After the last little while who could blame her? A
moment later Mariano comes in.

" This man, he left two others in the car by the
cantina." The big man informs me and goes to his
post in the kitchen.

" Show him in." I say with a flourish. Maybe he
wants to buy the place.

Leio Kei walks into the living room with quick
decisive step. While his size is diminutive his
attitude is one of dominance. There is a lot of
arrogance there but so what? He is a New Yorker.
And if he has anything of his father is self centered
as hell.

The face is child like, small, round and hard as a
chestnut. The features are small but the eyes look
through you. He stands there like he is giving me an

audience. Well we shall see about that.

" Mr. Kei would you care to sit down." I offer.

" No! Mr. McFurson I will stand. The business we will discuss should take a very little time." His English is reasonably good.

" Fine you have the floor." I agree. I don't want him here any longer than necessary.

" My father had some possessions which we have been unable to obtain. He owned this house some time ago. I wonder if anything has come to light which might help us to find these things." He waltzes.

" Your father took the possessions of people who were murdered. They call it the Chinese Mans treasure here. You must forgive them. It is very hard for them to identify Asians. As it would be difficult for you to identify a Cuban from say a Honduran. The point is the treasure is not here. You can see we are still filling in the deck from the last treasure hunt. Your father would never bring that much wealth down here. It's too hard to defend. I figure he was an intelligent man so it's in a bank somewhere." I say.

"Why would you say that?"

" Because I am a thinking man. Wealth is only relative if it is available. Parked under concrete requires a great deal of work to acquire it. In a bank it is easily in reach."

" You seem to have a lot of answers."

"Well you see I studied the matter. I've had my pool dug up I've been shot at and I'd like to live in the house I purchased without some idiot attempting to demolish it.  The treasure is not here and the explosion which was rigged to find it plus the destruction of my deck hasn't brought it to light. I would figure that would prove it isn't." I finish. He of course is not satisfied.

"It could be buried in the area." He states

" It might be but the water table is so high they entomb people or take them up the mountain to bury. Anything down here would be pushed to the surface. Your father's body guards went under cement to make sure they didn't surface. But you know that because some of the family had to be involved in the disposal." I finish.

" What happened then."

" Frankly. I don't care what happened then. That treasure comes from a holocaust. It doesn't belong to your father or your family. It belongs to the survivors of a decimated country."

" I will not argue possession,' He said convinced I didn't possess the money or know anything of value. 'However, should anything related to the matter be found I wish it to be given to me. If not, I can assure you life in this house would be impossible." I look into the eye's of someone who might have taken part in the killing fields, after all he was the right age, to whom life was less then cheep, especially when millions of dollars were involved.

Chapter Twenty , 10:00 Grand Central Station,
Montreal Quebec, Canada.

Search And Ye Shall Find.

The morning begins with two actions both are
required and both are difficult in their own way. I
am dropped off at a specific point and take a bus to
the Metro, Montreal's version of the underground
or subway. After doing the majority of the route and
finding I have a Cambodian attempting to follow
me a quick call to Marcel has him removed. As a
matter of fact the rest of Mr. Kei's group are
targeted and all of them are hauled in for good
measure. It seems there has been a lot of street
spitting going on, a filthy thing to do, the guns
found also were a concern so off they all went to be
questioned for hours. Mr. Kei himself is removed
from his warm hotel suite and also placed through
the wringer.

However, I take a cab anyway, then a second,
following that another bus for three blocks and then
the subway near Peel St. My twitch which is my
internal alarm system tells me when I am being
followed, at this moment it is quiet so I figure I am
in pretty good shape. I get to see the downtown
skyline once more the Place Ville Marie and other

memorable sights pass me by. McGill University, Sherbrook St. with its multiple bars and restaurants, the old Holt Renfrue Store and many others remind me of my youth and the joy I took in this great city. I remember in the East End one of my uncles not associated with the police taking me to a restaurant not much larger then a telephone booth with a grubby white painted counter and a plain presentation. However, the two nubile waitresses were naked from the waist up. The Food as I remember wasn't bad either.

Grand Central Station was built when our two major railways ran the passenger service and they made money from such endeavors. Now it is a hub for the VIA rail people who represent the government and have much less money along with a declining ridership. However new high speed trains in the Quebec to Windsor corridor are supposed to correct that problem. The station is built under a great hotel, is spacious, clean and used by millions as a central point for The Metro and the commuter trains which are still profitable. I enter from the interlocking underground shopping tunnels that connect most of the downtown core and wait for a while to see if anyone is around. My twitch is silent. Box 1239 is as plain as the rest with its' directions in both French and English printed boldly on the front. Behind me travelers are being called to descend to track level beneath where I stand to board the Maritimer leaving for Halifax and points East. I place the key in the lock almost expecting to hear the patter of running feet, or perhaps the stealthy tread just next to me followed with a gun in the ribs to take my victory away. Inside the small luggage box are eight envelopes. I remove one, lock the box and leave.

Mr. Kei senior was not without his wiles and the envelope poses a puzzle. There are two keys in the white envelope. One is a bank safety deposit box key but larger than I had ever seen before. Attached to it on the same ring was a smaller key probably to open the inside cover of the box. Folded neatly next to the keys was a short very clear sheet covered with what I suspected was Cambodian script. All oriental languages I am told are based on Chinese letters so it is very hard to identify one from another. The letter contains directions, no doubt, in code to where the treasure was hidden. I sat at the kitchen table in Marcel's comfortable house.

" We can give them the key then follow them to the object' I consider the thought, 'but I would really like to see this thing first."

"What is this thing worth?" Marcel asks for the first time. I had been expecting it.

" Not a great deal to the average person but it was tremendously important to millions at one time." You see I tell the truth. ' I wish I could read Cambodian."

"That's no problem we have a couple of those guys on the force now for public relations. They are good men I 'll ask one to show up after his shift.

Constable Lin Sheang sat across from me looking intently at the paper. He wrote what he saw as Marcel had requested. Police officers understand that information is always given out on a need to know basis.

" There is little here." he commented, "Just a number and some letters." He said tiredly.

" Thanks I think that is all I need.." The letters related to the bank, the number a personal identification code.

" The next morning was the first bank day after Christmas and the place was packed.
The Imperial Bank of British Columbia was a stately old structure. It was built around the turn of the century when bank buildings had class. There was the extra money for carved frescos and marble telling the potential client this was a safe and profitable place to invest. A huge new glass and

metal stereotype monolith ran its operations from across the street. The new central head office is in a twenty story building. It seems tall and ugly is in . However, this old stalwart structure was the repository for billions perhaps.

One enters through a marble lobby studded with cameras, passed busy cashiers, the well appointed branch offices until one comes to the steps to the underground vault. One's  number is required as if it is offensive to ask. This is provided and checked, a pleasant smile directs you to descend marble steps to the vault level. A hefty guard checks your key and you are allowed to enter the main vault. Here stacks upon stacks of safety deposit boxes stand row on row. Until those at the top which are smaller require movable ladders to reach them. The box I am taken to is on the ground. It's mouth is almost three feet across. I present my key and a duplicate is offered. The two turn and the box is partially pulled out. I blanch because I figure the guard and the secretary with him will see what is in the box . I forget the retracting metal cover which is opened with the second smaller key.

Both the guard and the secretary leave and close the vault door to insure my privacy. This section of the vault is for larger boxes and is separate from the smaller ones in the other room.

There are no cameras or none that my watch detects
but all the steel around it might have an effect.

The key works fine and I push the retracting
plates that cover the box back they silently compact
one on top of the other to show something uniquely
terrible. Oh! The treasure is there just as it was
stolen. Wrist watches, roles of money, objects of
gold and silver pieces of old armor looted no doubt
from museums. A bag of gold teeth partially
opened. Wedding rings hundreds of them spread on
top of the pile. There were bars of gold and a huge
selection of gems. I wondered if people had been
told if they cooperated and gave up what they had
that they would be spared. Money to finance the
revolution then your family can be reeducated to
farm. The information fearfully given. The reward
being a bullet in the back of the head. There were
bearer bonds as well. The hoard must have been
worth ninety or so million. Some of the artwork was
priceless.

I could not bring myself to touch it. For all it's
beauty it might have been manure for all I cared.
This was the hopes and dreams of a people. One
point seven million people who were butchered
while the world simply looked the other way and
forgot. All that was left of a generation of thinking
honest human beings lay in this coffin like box. Kie

wasn't going to get it, that was for sure. He had others behind him perhaps the old rulers perhaps others in the Oriental Triads who would take an interest. No this had to be handled with great subtlety. I wondered where one might find a great stubtleist on short notice. Sometimes humour is the only way to stay sane. I closed the box locked it and left.

Chapter Twenty One - 10:30 Pm , Louws
Restaurant, Sherbrook Street, Montreal Quebec.

To Trap A Fox.

Constable Lin Sheang sat comfortably drinking
green tea, watching his supporting cast which
included The esteemed  Mr.Kei Junior and two
others of his family. The muscle sat a few tables
away.

Mr. Kei is uncomfortable even though Lin has
been searched while holding his revolver over his
head in the men's room.

" You have a matter to discuss" Kei asks. Both
men speak Cambodian.

" If you have an interest in a key I do." Lin
offers.

" What key?"

" The key to something you want. McFurson is
family to that Lieutenant who keeps putting your
people in boxes. He thinks it's some kind of artifact
from the old land. That McFurson wants to find it
and return it to the generals back home. If it has any
value then it will go into their pockets. But they are
there you are here so for five thousand dollars I will
tell you where the key can be obtained."

" For five thousand dollars you will walk me into a trap." Lin shakes his head.

" You're an idiot. It has been an experience." He makes to leave.

" No! Police are not to be trusted here. Some are more honest than others. In the old land it is different."

" In that, cousin, you arc right.' Lin admits and sits back down.' Here's a good story. This McFurson is honest. He will do the right thing. He will give the key to the treasury board and someone from CICIS tomorrow. Then he expects the Canadian Government to get the object back to the Generals. The round eyes is too stupid to see things don't work the same here as there." He laughs and Kie smiles.

" If I knew where he was then I could take action ." Kei suggests, 'Does he have people with him he cares for?"

" Don't be an idiot. I have a good thing here I send you where he is. The department  will know because it is all family. You don't play ransom with the police, you aren't very bright.' Lin slows down, ' Listen cousin you are new to this up here so I will tell you what I can do. First this McFurson is moved from house to house, also he is some kind of cop. He has connections. The best time is at the meeting

because there are no Montreal police there. If
something happens that is not my problem.
McFurson has a bleeding heart he wants no trouble
only to get rid of the key. There will be only the
treasury guy and the CISIS one. That is all. The
CISIS guy has no gun. Just point a gun and take the
key it does not have to be you personally."

   " Yes this is true." Kie agrees but to have
anyone else handle the prize would be unthinkable.
" You take it." He says.

   " No cousin I will get you there but no further,
after that you have your own resources." Lin
indicates the men at the other table.' If it's too rich
for you. I understand."

   " I will give you Two thousand five hundred
now and the rest afterwards. If something goes
wrong I need not pay the rest. If all goes well you
get the remainder."

   " Cousin, five thousand dollars now or no deal."
Lin stands pat.

   " Four thousand. This is costing me a great
amount. Like McFurson said it only has value to
me. You cannot profit from it."

   Lin looks uncomfortable.

   " No five, I am putting a great deal forward on
this matter."

" Agreed!" Kei hisses. His left hand gestures. One of the family members hands Lin an envelope of the right size." Lin thumbs it just to make sure.

" My partner is outside so you try something after I tell this and you're dung." Lin snarls. 'The meeting will be in the old Dupont railway station in the East End at ten o'clock. There is a coffee shop with tables they will be sitting there. McFurson will come over give them the key and have a paper signed by the treasury man to cover himself. He will give them the key and that is all. Don't kill him. The round eyes' death will cause a lot of problems. His family will get involved. Good luck cousin."

I sit in a car with Marcel outside the station and wait for ten AM to occur.

" I don't want another one of these you understand?" Marcel is uncomfortable.

" I came here because it is the right place and you would help . A great general once said 'fight on your own ground.' If it was Central America or the Islands I would help. Anyway this is straight the government will have the object and will take care of it."

" Alright but don't get killed. I'd never hear the end of it from the family. Bien, its time to go."

" I get out of the car. The street is cleared and I know it. Two of my uncles stand by the door going in. I smile as I pass. The interior of the station is domed but grime had covered the glass to such an extent that only limited light gets in. This was a major send off point for the East End at one time but now it is only a commuter pick up. Of course there is a fair amount of traffic so it has a news stand, a drugstore attached and of course the inevitable coffee bar. Where at this very moment sits my friend Mr. Morningstar of CISIS and a guy who looks like an accountant. I figure him for Treasury. Morningstar looks nervous and my twitch is working over time so he probably has reason to.

The walk is short, the warmth of the building surrounds you as you leave the door. There is a low steel railing before the table I stand on the outside. I place the key on the table. All eight envelops are back in the luggage locker.

"There Mr. Morning Star is eight hundred million dollars, maybe more with inflation." I say to the astonished spy. 'It was stripped from the two million Cambodians killed in the seventies. I am sure you will see it gets back to that country safely. Please sign this paper it stipulates you have the key. The treasury guy starts to read like he is Rip Van Winkle. I notice action starting to my right and left. Then like the Calvary to the rescue I see Kie and his minions making a bee line for the table.

Sub-machineguns show under there clothing. I turn and walk away. The Treasury guy ducks under the table. Morningstar sits there like a deer in the headlight of an on coming freight. He will be alright though. I have taken care of everything. There are a number of soft popping noises. Kie's people stop as if they have had a unique idea and drop like sandbags. The RCMP are armed and the sedative in the air darts they use could knock out a moose. I am at the door. The dart aimed at Kie misses and a rather attractive young lady grabs her behind and then drops into dream land. Kie grabs the baggage key from the table. To Morningstar's credit he tries to stop him but its hard when you're seated behind a table which is being shoved into your gut by Kei's left hand. The little criminal turns and runs for the doors. One has been left open. Perhaps someone pushed it too hard and it has locked in place. The Cambodian stays low and the sharp shooters are nervous about putting some little old lady to sleep and her not waking up. Just as he makes the door and freedom, some mean minded two hundred and ten pound mother with a nasty sense of humor closes the door in the little man's face. There is an audible crunch as Kie's teeth collide with the metal mesh reinforced glass of the  polished hard wood door. I remove myself from my side of the door as

the Horsemen collect the struggling now bleeding
Kie  and relieve him of his prize. I get into the back
seat of the unmarked car while Marcel and the head
of the local RCMP detachment, who has stuck his
head outside the door, discus the weather for a
moment then we are off. Lin smiles at me from the
front seat. The microphone was in the gun of
course.

Chapter Twenty Three - !0:20 Am The Beach
Before McFurson's Castle, The Gulf Coast, Central
America.

A Blond On the Beach.

I walk along the sand slowly, stripped of
everything but a bathing suit, a flowered shirt and
my watch. I am free. At least for the moment. It is
true that some officials back in Canada wanted to
have me lynched or at least put through the grinder.
However, twenty four hours after checking into my
story they didn't want to know I existed. The
Treasury Board in it's own efficient manor sends
me a receipt for one baggage key of undetermined
origin.. I am allowed to leave. There are no travel
restrictions on coming back.

Given the uncompromising honesty of my
government I am assured that at this very moment
every sinew of the proper departments are working
at top speed to get that money back to it's rightful
owners. Also a small side bar in the Toronto Sun
about the incident placed by a friend helped
somewhat. At least everyone knows I don't have the
blood covered treasure and that is something.

Mr. Kei Junior is indicted on charges that he tried to
bribe an officer, attempted murder, possessing
stolen artifacts, assault on a federal officer in the
line, weapons charges and his extradition has been
requested by the Cambodian government in
connection with his action in the killing fields. It
seems the Generals were disappointed the elder Mr.
Kie wouldn't share his trove. Maybe the Canadian
diplomatic corps has something to do with it.

Marcel finds out what I have been hiding and won't
talk to me. In the end he comes around as do the
rest of the family because what I did was straight. I
will be invited back to Christmas again next year.

An article in the Roman Catholic Monthly tells of
a twelve million dollar gift from a blind trust to the
Sisters of the Redemption. The good sisters run a
number of medial missions in Cambodia through
their mother house in the City of Rouen in France.
Part of the bequest was a used CAT scan donated by
a US Military hospital in Santa Lucinius California
and a wide range of medical equipment including a
large number of  surplus medical beds from a
hospital in Kitchener Ontario Canada. It seems that
thousands of Cambodian lives were being saved by
this wonderful bequest.

It is truly amazing how God works his miracles.

Old Dell has won his war but looks like he will be
in the Middle East for a while. I say a prayer for
him when I can.

Big Mouth Fish tells me both Dr. Pope and Pat are
doing fine. I never hear what happens to Pat but I
hope they treat him well. Pat did his job even
though I almost died because of it.

Wordless Phil got that heap of a helicopter back to
the British Virgins. Someone must be watching over
him.

Tomas will go to school in Canada living with my
relatives. I have adopted him and he will do well.
Sanchez's dream is helped I guess by my action but
the average Latino is hard working and does the
best he can with what he has. They have no interest
in harming anyone. They don't want to take over
they just want to make the place they have better.

All is well I guess. I have done something for
mankind. Rightly, wrongly, perhaps stupidly but my
unfailing luck seems to have kept me alive and out

of trouble. However, I don't want to test it too much more.

Turner, Peachy and the crew back in London don't know about Montreal nor should they. It has nothing to do with them. I only tell them I have cleared up my treasure mess which is true. Right now they have lots on their plates. If they ask I will be honest. I am afraid to think what Turner will do if he finds out about all that money he missed out on but I am retired and the money belongs to the Cambodians. I hope they benefit from it. They sure haven't got much else from the world.


I see her coming down the beach from a distance. She is just a cloud of blond hair blowing in the wind which has picked up. We will of course be having more rain and this cooling zephyr is a precursor of it's coming.

Shylow has returned. I am overjoyed to see her but try to play it a little cool after all. Women like the objective to be a little hard to get.

She smiles and waves, her green eyes shine with deviltry, then begins to take her clothes off. The Jazz Lady is naked by the time we reach each other. Shylow's pert little breasts point excitedly at me, her hard well cared for body with all its defects makes me respond. I like her and perhaps love her. What can I say? Thank you God for sending her back to me. I need her and she in some real way needs me. It's a start!

"Hi!" is all she says and walks out into the surf. I shed my clothing and follow the soft . sway of her firm flat bum out into the waves. We swim and make love in the sea her body arching from me relying on her legs wrapped around my waist to balance her as she climbs her mountain then trembles into fulfillment. As the sun sets we walk back to the house. I carry her bag up from the cantina .

There is no friction between the two women. After all I am the master of this place and there is a job to consider. There is no recrimination though perhaps a little sadness..

Shylow is tired she needs some space. We live together comfortably making no undo demands on each other. Perhaps we will marry, if so it will be when we want too. My world is full again after much turmoil. We talk and make music together and do all the little things that drive each other  nuts but does not for some reason break up the relationship.

I make peace with my wife and move on as she would have liked me to. I will not go out again for the Firm but then I am the local rep on the books and still receive my pension. Never say never. But I do not want this idyllic time endangered or to be damaged because of my past life, for the moment I am content.

## END IT

### McFurson Will Return
### in  Why Not

This novel is pure fiction. The Characters do not
exist. The situations are strictly for the amusement
of the reader, these events have no substance in
reality and have never happened.
While locations do exist they are only backdrops.
Any references to people living or dead and any
likeness to those persons is strictly coincidental

Thank you for reading my book
George V. Henderson

# FROM THE PUBLISHER

georgev_henderson@hotmail.com